Heike Brandt would like to thank the Deutscher Übersetzerfonds e.V for the scholarship which enabled her to come to Australia.

Allen & Unwin
83 Alexander St
Crows Nest NSW 2065
Australia
Phone: (61 2) 8425 0100
Fax: (61 2) 9906 2218
Email: info@allenandunwin.com
Web: www.allenandunwin.com

National Library of Australia
Cataloguing-in-Publication entry:

Honey, Elizabeth, 1947– .
To the Boy in Berlin.
ISBN 978 1 74175 004 1
1. Justice, Administration of – Juvenile fiction. 2. Detective and mystery stories, Australian. I. Brandt, Heike, 1947– . II. Title.
A823.3

Cover design by Elizabeth Honey and Ruth Grüner
Text design by Ruth Grüner
Set in 10.3 pt Metaplus Book / 9.3 pt Courier by Ruth Grüner
Printed and bound in Australia by Griffin Press

1 3 5 7 9 10 8 6 4 2

Teacher's notes available from www.allenandunwin.com

ELIZABETH HONEY
& HEIKE BRANDT

TO THE BOY IN BERLIN

ALLEN&UNWIN

For Sal and Kez
E.H.

Para Tania y Miguel
H.B.

In books lies the soul
Of the whole past time
The articulate audible voice of the past
When the body
And material substance of it
Has altogether vanished like a dream

THOMAS CARLYLE (1795–1881)

I like to invent people. When we were little I told my sister Danielle that a witch lived under her bed, and if she closed her eyes the witch would talk to her. So Danielle shut her eyes tight, and I slipped under her bed – '*WooOOoo! HellooOo Daanieelle, this is Haggy BabaNeeeema!*'

My Grade 2 teacher wrote on my report 'Henni tends to fabricate', which Mum said meant 'likes making things'. I invented Big and Little, Dimmy Dishling, a cousin called Gordie with whooping cough and lockjaw (at the same time!). I dealt out luck and tragedy, but as I got older my stories went down on paper.

But I did not invent Leopold. He was real. And Leopold made things happen – boy, did he make things happen!

I discovered
Leopold last Easter.
We were staying in
an old wooden house
high up in the trees at
a remote beach. That house had
a fresh living-outside feeling, yet
in the storm, when the branches
thrashed like a wild sea, we felt safe.
We wanted to know who had built
the house. Whoever they were, we
liked them a lot.

First we found German board
games, and then a measuring place
behind the kitchen door, with
children's heights marked in pencil:
Gretel, Christa, and the tallest,
Leopold. That was the first time
I read his name. We found a
wooden platform high in a
towering gum tree. We found
out Konrad Schmidt, a German
furniture-maker, built the house
round the time of the First
World War; his wife, Bettina,
was sick; there was no school, but
a local lady taught the Schmidt kids with her kids;
and Leopold, who was about my age, taught himself from
books. I liked that bit.

Actually, I was feeling extremely left out last Easter.
My best friend had brought another friend, and I had to
look after an awful new girl who came to stay with us.
I imagined Leopold – the eldest, like me – would have had a
hard time too, being responsible for his sisters and his poor
sick mother.

The Schmidts' story was mysterious because one day
they suddenly left Cauldron Bay, never to return. I wanted
to know where they went and what happened to Leopold.
Their possessions were still under the house, including three
boxes of books,
so, when we were
packing up, I
slipped down
(with everyone
scuffling and
thumping on
the floor above)
and I tucked
this note into
a dusty box.
It was like
launching a
message in
a bottle.

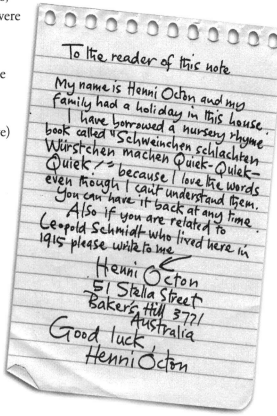

To the reader of this note

My name is Henni Octon and my
family had a holiday in this house.
I have borrowed a nursery rhyme
book called "Schweinchen schlachten
Würstchen machen Quiek-Quiek-
Quiek!" – because I love the words
even though I can't understand them.
You can have it back at any time.
Also if you are related to
Leopold Schmidt who lived here in
1915 please write to me.
        Henni Octon
        51 Stella Street
        Baker's Hill 3771
                Australia
Good luck,
Henni Octon

Last thing before we left, us kids lined up behind the kitchen door and marked our modern heights beside the heights of the 1914 German kids. I remember thinking, I'm taller than you, Leopold.

Then, yesterday, this arrived . . .

Dieter Kramer
Kreuzberger Stadtteilgeschichte in 10 Postkartenserien
Serie 8: Der Kreuzberg
Nr. 824: Yorck-, Ecke Großbeerenstraße, um 1910 (Slg. Landehennig). Deutlich erkennbar ist die großzügige Gestaltung der Yorckstraße als Boulevard: Ein begrünter Mittelstreifen als Promenade und Vorgärten vor den Häusern, die häufig von Cafés und Gaststätten genutzt wurden, zum Beispiel vom 'Yorckschlößchen', einem Gartenlokal – rechts, an der Ecke zur Hornstraße – das bis heute unter demselben Namen existiert. Die Großbeerenstraße wurde 1864 nach der Schlacht bei Großbeeren während des 'Befreiungskrieges' 1813 benannt.

PORTA NIGRA TRIER
1,00 €
DEUTSCHLAND

LUFTPOST
PAR AVION PRIORITAIRE

Henni Oxton
51 Stella Street
Baker's Hill 3771
AUSTRALIA

Berlin, 26. August
Dear Henni Oxton!

Am I related to Leopold Schmidt if I am Leo Schmidt? My uncle Sascha gave me Abnode you left with the books saying: Isn't that nice coincidence? Keep the nursery rhyme: Jam Durken and prefer novel. The postcard shows my neighbourhood a hundred year ago close to 1975. It's Yorckstraße. If you want to write: leo.schmidt@berlin.de
Tschüs! Leo

Melbourne, Wednesday 31 August 5.02pm

LEO SCHMIDT!!!!!!!!!!!!!!!!!!!!!!!!!!!!!!!!

You're joking!
Are you joking?
You are.
And you're in Berlin!
Ordinary ordinary ordinary breakfast school homework ordinary ordinary ordinary ***postcard from Berlin!!!***

JeepersLeo! I thought it would be sixty years before my note was discovered, not six *months*!

How did your uncle get my note? Are you related to the 1915 Leopold Schmidt and do you know what happened to the Schmidts when they left Cauldron Bay? I know Schmidt is Smith and it's a common name, but this is one big fat coincidence.

Thanks for the postcard. Is the arrow your house? I'm looking at it through a magnifying glass. The avenue is grand and peaceful with horses and carriages. The couple on the left are going to buy the children a dachshund, and the lady crossing the tram tracks has decided to sack the cook because she coughs on the soup. We had trams like that in Melbourne. We still have trams. Do you?

What's Tschus? A sneeze?
Answer soon LEO SCHMIDT in Berlin
if that's who you are

Henni Octon

pinching herself

Hi Henni — no jokes on my side. I am Leo Schmidt. The one and only. Well, I checked the Berlin phone book and found four other Leo Schmidts — in nineteen pages of Schmidts. About 10 000 people!!! But that must be the adult ones, because kids don't have an entry in a phone book, right? Even though most kids have a telephone, mobile, I mean. I don't. My friends call me the Dinosaurus of Communication. I do emails, don't I?

No Leopold Schmidt in the phone book. Well, your Leopold lived long ago. How old was he in 1915? There is no Leopold in my family — at least no one my mother knows. And it would have to be on my mother's side, because my parents are not married and I carry my mother's family name.

But I think there is a way to find your Leopold Schmidt — with the Small-World-Hypothesis. My Uncle Sascha, the one who found your note, explained it to me: everybody is connected to any other person in the world over six degrees of separation. You can find interesting details in the internet. But I don't know if it works backwards, I mean back into history. Hmm.

You fired a lot of questions.

No trams anymore in this part of town. The two corner houses on the left have been destroyed during the war. The corner house on the right is still there. No, we don't live where the arrow is. We live behind the pub, in another street, which is not on the picture. You sure have a wild imagination.

I have only one question: who are you? Never heard the name Henni. It's almost German — if you change the last letter to an e you have Henne, which is hen. So I guess you are female?

Ach so: Tschüs is German for goodbye!

Are you going to answer even though I am not the Leopold you were looking for? (2. question) I have never met anyone from "down under". I swear I am not thinking anymore that you people live upside down, feet on the ground, head dangling in the air.

You are probably sleeping now — or getting up, or going to school — or is it the other way round? My watch shows 5.58 in the afternoon, August 31.

Bye for now, Leo

Good morning or good night or good whatever it is,
LeoSchmidtfromBerlin

Yes, I am disappointed. I wanted one degree of separation
not six. I hoped to find out about my mysterious Leopold
Schmidt. I think he was about thirteen in 1914, which is another
super-colossal coincidence because I'm thirteen, same as you.

How did your uncle get my note? I left it under the house
where Leopold and his family lived. We stayed there last Easter.
It had been locked up for ages but we sure woke it up   Hang
on! I have to yell at my sister! She's bashing a tennis ball
against the back wall and she just hit my bedroom window
again!!!!!

I'm back!

The house at Cauldron Bay. We loved all the clever bits of
building and the big fireplace and the way it was high up, like
a ship in the trees. Underneath, it was like in the movies, where
they break the curtain of cobwebs to enter the tomb of treasure!
There were boxes of old German books but I didn't get a chance
to look at them.

Can you email from your own computer? I have to use my dad's.

I do have a most Faithful Intelligent computer of my Own
called Byron but he can't speak Email.

She hit my window *AGAIN!!!!!*

Everything's hitting this place at the moment. Dad's
thumping around because I messed up his desk when I went
on his computer – just shoved his papers to one side so I could
put my breakfast down. And Mum's new job at the medical

11

clinic might be good for other people's health but it's not good for ours right now. Then there's my sister Danielle, who is ten – Australia's next great tennis champ, according to Dad.

I know German: mercedes benz, kindergarten, kinder, garten, Ya, Nein, Achtung! Volkswagen, Tschus . . .

How come you are so good at English?

Nice talking to you, Dinosaurus of Communication.

Now I want to know about Leopold Schmidt AND Leo Schmidt.

NO MORE SCHMIDTS!!!!!!!!!!!!!!

Yours sincerely

Henni

Hi Henni,

My Uncle Sascha found your note, yes, under a house. He was in Australia to shoot a documentary film about surfing. He is the most curious person in the world. If anyone was to find your note, it was him. He even asked one of the locals, a motorbiker, about your Leopold Schmidt. Only he got shoved off with: "Leave the dead alone." Sascha didn't have more time then, but I bet you he would have tried to find out more. He and Tania, his girlfriend and director, are always exploring places — caves and old castles and wrecked factories and shattered houses and lonesome lakes - whatever. And they always bring me a gift: the tooth of a horse, a stone with a face on it, a little marble figure with no head, a rusty iron iron. I have a big collection of things on a special shelf — and your note is now part of it. First item from Australia.

My friend Felix just entered. Now he's slumped onto my bed and goes: "So — you have a pen pal?" With a foolish grin on his face. Grrr.

Actually he isn't so bad. Belongs to the French gang in school. And we were both in the same class at elementary school. I know him since we were six. He loves riddles and knows hundreds of them. And he is a great chess player.

I rather play on a wider field, more globally.

Soccer that is.

Leo

P.S. Felix asks: "Hey Australia — do you play chess?"

Okay, your turn to move.

Hello Leo,

I'd love to see Sascha's film of the surfies. It's amazing that Sascha and Tania even found Cauldron Bay because the surfies chop down the signposts to keep it a secret. We have a TV channel, SBS, which shows stuff from other countries. Their film might be on that.

What did that biker mean by 'Leave the dead alone'? Leopold *is* dead. He'd be over a hundred if he was alive now. Creepy!

Hello Felix! No, I don't play chess.

(I know about people watching everything you do. At school I am a new weird species discovered by this girl Cherelle and her trusty bunch of fleabrains. I can feel their eyes on me. I am *so* entertaining.)

Yours sincerely

up beside the rusty iron iron

Henni

  the girl

    not the hen

P.S. When do you use capital letters in German? There's an awful lot of them.

I like the Germanjoinedupwords on the back of the postcard. What's the longest word you know?

Berlin, Freitag, 2.September 20.46

Hi Henni. I have thought about your problem
with your Dad and emailing. Why don't you write
your letters on your computer, save them on disc
or diskette and then mail them from your Dad's
computer? Saves stress, too.

Just noticed that you send your last email at
6.10pm — my computer registered it at 10.11 in
the morning, while I was sitting in Math! So you
must be eight hours ahead of us? Now it's almost
9 o'clock and slowly getting dark. Which means
you are sleeping, already in September third?

Read you! Leo

P.S. The longest word? In German you can add
nouns to compose a new one, like tree house
= **Baumhaus. Baum = tree, -haus = house.** If
you need a key for the tree house it would be
Baumhausschlüssel.

Some nice ones:

**Donaudampfschifffahrtsgesellschaftsraddamp
ferkapitänskajütentürsicherheitsschlüssel**: the
security key of the captain's cabin door of
the Danube shipping company.

Heizölrückstoßabdämpfung: this is the longest
word without repetition of a letter — some
technical stuff about fuel oil.

Holyjamrolly!   Can you *say* those words?

Email you on disc. Brilliant!!!
Dad's happy – I'm off his computer. He's taught me to scan.
But bad news for you – my emails will be longer ! ! !
Can't talkj now. Late
Tel me aboutyou.

About me?

Hmm. It's Monday evening, nothing on TV. Lotte, my little sister (turning five this month and no tennis player yet!!!), is sound asleep, parents are out. Unusual silence. Almost like fishing. When you sit with your bait and wait.

Only now I am sitting in my room at my desk with my new computer. Birthday present. I can go online any time.

In the mirror I see a boy with short blond curly hair (way too curly, that's why I want it short), wearing glasses. It was just recently that we discovered I need them. Now I really see the ball before I catch it. Amazing. I play goalkeeper on the soccer field. Problem is, I am pretty short. What else? I have a bruise on my forehead. I bumped into an overhanging branch riding my bike this weekend.

We were at our Datsche — summerhouse. It's in the former East Germany. We lease a plot close to a lake just outside Berlin. Knut, my Dad, wants to build a wooden house (he is a carpenter) but we haven't got the money yet. So we sleep in a little shack. It's great out there. Because I can go fishing (which comes right after soccer).

This time it was a bit dull because Felix didn't come, although he had promised. He didn't show up at leaving time. Then I called him and his mother said, no, Felix won't come. No explanation. Wonder what he did to get grounded. In school he didn't say much. I even think that he kind of avoided me.

Antek got beaten up today, and Felix kept out of it. Very unusual. Felix always speaks up if anything goes wrong. But not this time. I didn't see the fight, but Mustafa told me what happened.

Antek had said something about Islam being an aggressive religion — the jihad and the terrorists and all that. Then Ali shot back and asked him what about the crusades? When the Christians killed Muslims in the name of God? And what about the pope! How could a human being be the deputy of God on earth? Then Ali and Ozan and Khaled made jokes about the pope, and boing! Antek got mad and fists flew — only they were three and he was one. Felix just went away. By the time Mustafa got there, Antek was on the ground with a bleeding nose.

I hate this religion stuff. Antek is okay, but he is very, very Catholic. There is a big church close to our school, only used by the Polish community. They have services all in Polish. The new mosque with golden minarets is a little further away. And next to it is a big cemetery with a section for Muslims. The graves are put from east to west, in rows, with Arabic letters sometimes. And close by are huge memorials of German soldiers of the last three big wars. At least they can all share a cemetery.

I don't believe in God. Do you?

This is a new school I am going to — 7th Grade.
Big school, a comprehensive school. I am lucky
because I have friends. There is Felix. And
Mustafa, who lives in my street. We play soccer
in the same team. He is a fabulous striker. On
the field. Outside he is rather peaceful, though
you don't want to mess with him. Antek is a new
friend. He looks much older than us, but he is
also thirteen. He plays guitar — his parents
think he is studying classic guitar, but actually
it's rock music he is doing. He joined the school
band. And he is a magician. He taught me some
tricks and now Lotte thinks I have supernatural
powers!

Your German sounds great, though I may
suggest a few corrections: it's not "ya" but
"ja" (pronounced like ya). And it's tschüs and
not tschus: the "tsch" is pronounced like "tsh"
(imagine a steam train!) and the "ü" like the
"ui" in "juice". And in German all nouns (Kinder,
Garten) begin with a capital letter.

My English? When I was a year old, my parents
put me in our neighbor's care. She is from the
U.S. and used to run a little nursery school
in her flat. So my parents thought: it won't
hurt Leo to learn English. Now I only get to
practice it in school. We have a bi-lingual
English course. But I am the only bi-lingual one
— in English that is. There are many bi-lingual
kids — they speak German and Turkish/Arabic/
Polish/Italian ... only that doesn't give them

any credits in school. I picked up some Turkish.
It's fun to exchange infos during a test, and the
teacher doesn't get it!

See you later? Leo

SO LEO SCHMIDTINBERLIN . . .
You are short and blind. Hmmm . . . I think you are telling
the truth.

Well here's me: if us people 'down under' did live hanging
upside down I'd be even more of a landmark than I am already,
because I'm tall and I also have very long hair. Unfortunately a
landmark has to be responsible, which I don't always feel like
being.

I got the name Henni when I was little. I fell in a drain and
one of my favourite books was about Hendrika, a Dutch cow
who fell in a canal. So, while they were trying to rescue me, my
parents joked and called me Hendrika, which turned into Henni.
Danielle calls my room Henhenge, and my friend Zev calls me
Hendecahedron or Hentathlon or Henultimate. And Dad used
to call me Hunda-bun-buncher, which came from Hun from Hen,
and my English teacher Miss Dakin calls me Henrahen.

But most people call me Henni.

When you said 'I hate this religion stuff' that shocked me
because I talk to God a lot. And another thing that shocked
me was Antek getting beaten up. I know religion gets people
mad. In Australia, religion used to be *very* strong – Dad said
the Catholics (Micks) and the Protestants (Prodos) hated each
other's guts, but now it's the Muslims who are copping it.

When I was little I believed in heaven, angels, pearly gates,
the lot. Every Sunday Grandma used to take Danielle and me to
church (which I now think was so Mum and Dad could sleep in).
But . . . God? I don't know anymore . . .

I do pray to God and I ask him to help me, and when things are really good I want to thank someone, so I thank God. And when I'm in deep trouble I pray to God, and sometimes I sort of gossip to God. I like to talk out loud. Maybe God is just me talking to myself, or an imaginary friend?

But I do know this: my God isn't in a church, that's for sure.

I'm jealous of you having good friends because I don't. (A strong Turk like Mustafa could be handy too!) Oh, school's okay, I'm not slashing my wrists, but primary school was fun, like a family – we never had to think about what we said or did, and my best friend Zev went there too. But Zev won a science scholarship to another high school.

When I started here in January I made a big mistake. I stuck up for this girl, Selma, who was being picked on because she blinks a lot. Now divine Cherelle and the Cherellettes peck at me too.

There is a girl, Athena, I'd like to be friends with. She's nice but scatty and changeable. When we talk it feels sparky and unpredictable. I think she could have lots of friends but she hasn't decided who yet.

I know one person likes me – Miss Dakin, my English teacher. She recommends great books. She says there's a project in the pipeline that I will love, but she won't tell me more so I won't be disappointed if it doesn't happen.

About capital letters in German, is it like 'The Alligator ate the Man in the Bath'?

I'll look for the two dots in Word but not now.

Sneaking off to Dad's computer to send this by the new method.

Tschus missing its dots

Henni
P.S. Doing anything interesting this weekend?
What was up with Felix?

meDownUnder.jpg

Hi Henni, when I read your mail yesterday I felt
like reacting immediately. As if a ball was
coming towards my goal. Only yesterday I had a
lot of homework and then soccer training — when
you miss training you don't get to play in
the match on Saturday. A new guy showed up.
A goalkeeper. Taller than I am. Much taller.
If he joins, my days as goalkeeper might be over.
Well, you might not be interested in soccer.

Or are you???

School was out early today, a sick teacher or
something. My Mom is working this afternoon — she
works in a bookstore. My Dad is in his workshop.
He'll pick up Lotte from kindergarten and won't
be home before six. So I am all on my own, turned
on *AC/DC* — LOUD — and NOW I can talk to you.
Are you there? Sleeping or awake? Tell me what
you do when I get up, let's say, seven in the
morning — my time.

You said you were shocked that Antek had
been beaten up. So was I. But he was the one who
started the whole thing. So in a way he had it
coming. But three on one is not fair.

I am not baptized, never went to church.
My Mom used to read the Bible or the Koran to me
when she explained what Easter and Christmas or
Ramadan or Hanukkah was about. I got the feeling
that religion is like a good goodnight story.
Lotte never goes to sleep without a long story.

26

First a picture book, then a made-up story. And
she tells you exactly what she wants in it. Once
she wanted a real scary one. I invented something
with a mummy that came back to life. That was
scary! Her teeth rattled! Then last week she told
me: "Leo, you can't scare me anymore! Because
mummies can't get up. If they do, they fall into
dust!"

Yes, I am lucky I have friends. Mustafa by
the way is German. He was born here, and both his
parents too. He doesn't believe in God — Allah
either. His grandparents come from Turkey. His
Grandpa was a shepherd in Anatolia. When he
was eighteen Germany was recruiting workers for
their factories, so he left his village and came
to Berlin. He thought to stay just a few years,
but never went back. Only to get married. And
for holidays. He is a funny guy with a white
moustache and a big tummy (from too much beer,
says Mustafa) and he speaks a funny German. They
run a grocery store, the whole family. When I
visit and help out, it's fun. But Mustafa has
to do it all the time. That's different. He is
definitely not going to sell groceries for the
rest of his life.

What's with Felix? Don't know. I asked him
about the weekend and he mumbled he was sorry,
but he just couldn't make it — his parents needed
him. I have no idea, and don't dare to ask why he
is so quiet. Still helping me in Math though. He
really is a brain, but when it comes to practical

life he is impossible. His fingers can only think when they move chess figures on the board.

Maybe his Dad lost his job? But he would tell me that. There are six kids in class whose parents don't have a job, so that's rather normal.

Could it be his parents want to split up?

My parents did that, when I was three. I don't remember it though. They separated for over a year. Knut had his own flat, where I had a room. I have seen pictures of that time but I just cannot remember it. They say it was a tough time for me.

Maybe that is bothering Felix and he is too embarrassed to talk about it. Would I tell him if my parents were splitting up? Dunno

The weekend. First soccer, then maybe Datsche. Nothing special.

Okay. Tschüs! Leo

You can find the letter "ü" on the special character menu!

Berlin, Donnerstag, 8.September 21.55

HENNI — back again. Got to talk to you.

Something strange happened.

Don't know what to do.

I had just sent your mail when the door bell rang. Maik walked in.

We are not friends or anything and he didn't explain why he came. That guy sure is different. When we had the first meeting of our new class, he was sitting on his father's lap! Everybody kind of looked, but nobody said a thing. My Mom told me he is a foster child. His mother can't take care of him because she is drinking, and a father doesn't exist, at least not for Maik. In class he is always playing the clown, and sometimes he really is funny. In French the teacher asked him to do the nasal sound, and Maik farted! With the most innocent face he explained that he had understood he should do an anal sound. He often gets thrown out, then the foster parents get called to school. He has no friends because he can get real mean. You say something wrong and you have had it. So most of us keep clear of him.

Okay, there he was. We went into my room, and he looked at everything as if he was in a store and couldn't decide what he should buy. Even opened drawers. I got nervous. Then he wanted something to drink and I went to the kitchen and got some apple juice. When I came back he was reading my comics, and he got annoyed that I didn't have Coke. Then he left. Strange.

Half an hour ago I checked my money because I plan to buy a new fishing rod — and you know what? The 50 Euro bill I had in the top drawer of my desk, in an envelope, present from Sascha, was gone!! The envelope was empty!!!

Now: do you think what I think?

Do I think this because Maik is a foster child? And if he did, what do I do to get the money back? Do I ask him? And if he didn't do it, what will he think of me?

Shit.

Don't even know if I can tell my Mom. She hates it when people get "put into drawers", as she calls it: foster child = thief, for example.

Boy, this gives me the creeps! That's not the kind of riddle I like to solve.

Read you,

Leo

That is AWFUL!

BUTAre you *sure* the money is gone?

Absolutely 100% ***POSITIVE***   ?

Check, check, check and check because things happen that you can't imagine. At Cauldron Bay a girl came to stay with us and I didn't like her. Then, for my birthday I was given a silver propelling pencil and when it disappeared I was *positive* she'd taken it. And you know who took my pencil?

A *bird* !

A bowerbird took it for his bower.

I was totally wrong.

So ***check!!*** Is it a jammedinjumblejunk drawer? Is it stuck to something else? Could it slip down the back? Maybe you took it out and forgot? Maybe someone borrowed it. Parents sometimes need more cash in a hurry.

Before you make Maik an enemy, be as sure as you can. I've decided people always think the worst.

Maik sounds weird – funny, like a kid in a comic. Anyone who sits on his father's lap when he's our age is *seriously* strange!

It *is* a lot of money – that's about $90 – Aussie dollars.

Now I'm mad at Maik too, because he derailed my news.

Miss Dakin has set the end of year project. It's *great!* December, the end of the school year here, is always a slack time because teachers are marking exam papers and writing reports. You still have to go to school, but kids sit around playing cards or chess or watching movies. If you're Cherelle you get a new boyfriend, that kind of thing. Parents complain because they always want you to be LEARNING, so the teachers have cooked up this project.

With a partner we pick a topic, then we go and stay with friends or relatives to research it. For example, if you're doing the gut-spilling sea urchin you go and stay with your uncle, the world-famous marine biologist.

We have to think up questions, draw up forms, and finally do a presentation and write a report.

Here's what I'm hoping – Leopold Schmidt's story. With Athena

Soccer's okay but I don't know anything about it. I'm in the Year 7 debating team but we haven't done much because Mr Walton's sick.

You have a BOOKSHOP MOTHER! Lucky thing!

Mum said when I was little I used to play bookshops. I would drag a chair over to the bookcase, for a counter, and ask baby Danielle if she liked puppies or elephants, then I'd sell a book (to myself) and buy it (from myself, with old tram tickets) and read it to Danielle . . . Well, I couldn't actually *read* it, but Mum says I used to say the story in a reading sort of way.

Mum's new job is getting more intense. Danielle and I are copping a crash course in cooking. More like crash and burn! Last night the roast wasn't cooking fast enough so I put it on the top shelf, because hot air rises, and turned up the gas. Then it burnt! All that work getting the vegetables ready and they ended up like sinister volcanic rocks. We ate the good bits. Danielle was snaky but *she* can't talk, yesterday she burnt the tacos black in fifteen minutes flat!

The attachment – here's me when you're springing out of bed at 7am! Everyone's asleep, so here I go, tiptoe, to send this.

Henni

MY Schedule.jpg

YES I am absolutely positive. The money is gone.
I DID CHECK!!! OVER AND OVER AND OVER AGAIN!
N O T H I N G ! ! !

I did ask Bettina and Knut (innocently looking) if they had ever borrowed money from me. And both said (kind of upset) they would never ever search in my drawers, not to mention take things — why are you asking, is anything missing? No, no ...

I also searched my brain. Did I spend the money? Did I put it some other place? But the envelope is still there! When I got the money, Lotte drew a picture of an old man on the envelope. "He collects money," she said. Probably she had seen a beggar.

Anyway, I took all drawers completely out to see if the money was stuck someplace. I looked at every possible place — **NO** 50 Euro bill. I did find the sock I'd been missing for quite a while, plus my soccer-club membership card, which my trainer had been asking for since ages. BUT NO MONEY. Bettina wanted to know why I had this orderly fit ... Luckily I could present the missing membership card.

And to make it worse. **MAIK HAS GOT NEW SNEAKERS! BRAND NEW CONVERSE!**

First thing I saw when I got to school this morning.

Is this proof enough?

34

Your project sounds great. You mean you get to visit someplace and do what you are interested in? That doesn't sound like school. Even though you have to make a report. Athena? Is she a goddess???

What is a gut-spilling sea urchin??? Who is throwing up what? My dictionary says: urchin = homeless child, naughty boy.

Even Bettina has no clue. Yes, it is nice to have access to many books. I love to read. And I love it when Bettina reads to me before I go to sleep. She does it once or sometimes twice a week. We choose the book together and afterwards we talk about what she's read. Just the two of us. It takes us long before we are finished with one book. But I wouldn't want to miss it.

Well, I'd better go now. Homework. No project. Math. Percentage Calculation. Fun factor: 0%. Wish Felix would be here to help me, but he hasn't come round since I wrote the first letter to you. In school he is very, very quiet. Like a volcano. Today in Biology class he exploded. Maik had been called to the blackboard to sketch a system of insect control, but drew a condom instead. We snickered, but the teacher got mad and sent him out of the classroom to "cool off". Felix jumped up and yelled: "You think it's a solution to throw out people who don't fit? Eliminate them?" The teacher just gave him a stern look and said: "I think this is completely beside the point. You can join Maik, if you want

35

to." So Felix got up and left the classroom!

Woops — Knut has just come into my room to ask me
when we will be going to buy the new fishing rod.
I said next week or so. I swear I saw two big
question marks in his eyes! I was the one who got
on his nerves: "Let's go and buy it, let's go."
I was mad because he was so busy. But tonight
I didn't feel like telling him the Maik story.
    Are you still listening, letter-box friend?
    Waiting for your answer. (I didn't think this
would happen when Sascha gave me your note.)
    Leo

P.S. Thanks for the picture. Now I know how you
look not hanging. And how hours fly by (I have
always wondered how this happens ...)

Melbourne, Wednesday 14 September 5pm

Rsz*bCDZX zdddd903* ⟨···· me collapsing on keyboard from starvation

Just got your email. Back in ten minutes. Don't go away!

Mmmmmm, Nutella!!!!!!!

Now, LeoSchmidtinBerlin, this is serious!

So Maik is wearing your fishing rod on his feet. What are our options?

Declare war and fight him to the death	possible but messy, fatal?
Anoymous threat	cowardly
Call for The Judge	Principal, teacher, United Nations – telltale wimpy
Call for reinforcements	Antek, Mustafa, army, air force – possible but not noble
Casually attach him to a lie detector	tricky
Steal his sneakers and use them to fish	satisfying but complicated
Tell parents	major escalation, lectures, *arggghh!*
Become best friend and gently point out problem	very long-term, impossible?

BUT remember the pencil-stealing bird! We need **_PROOF!!!_**

What if you show him the envelope with the beggar on it and say, 'Maik, can I have a *CONVERSE*ation with you?'

If he is guilty and you don't stand up to him he'll just do it again. He thinks he's got away with it.

We need PROOF!!!!

Talking of proof — — — — — —

$$|$$
$$|$$
$$V$$

Your mother's name is Bettina?!?!?!? And your father is a carpenter!?!?

Leopold Schmidt's mother was Bettina. And his father made furniture!?!?!?

I am suspicious again.

If you're pulling my leg I'll . . . . . . think of something . . . at least your father's name isn't Konrad . . . although Knut starts with a K!?!?!?!

No, Athena is not a goddess, but her parents did come from Athens. She asks wild questions that make me laugh, like, 'Can I do a slide point power projector show?' She could be a genius

or not

ANYWAY

At lunchtime yesterday there was a bunch of us girls sitting on the steps of the gym near the oval (Cherelle & co used to sit there but now they sit on the steps of the new science block near the boys toilets). I was telling Athena about some book, when I plucked up courage and said, 'Have you got a partner for the project yet?'

'No.'

'I've got a great topic that would be fantastic to do. It's the true story of a German family who migrate to Australia just before the First World War, to an isolated wild location, but for some unexplained reason they suddenly leave. A journey of migration, hope, isolation . . .'

'History?' she said, as if she was saying 'Brussels sprouts!'

'Well, sort of . . .'

My story lost its sparkle and I heard myself sounding rather desperate. I felt awful because I'd made the Schmidts' lives into some cheap novel.

Athena said, 'I've got a couple of ideas for the project' – then the bell rang.

Saved by the bell? Dunno. At least we're talking.

I thought about Felix too. Remember that girl I blamed for my missing pencil? Her parents were separating. She was *totally* screwed up.

My turn to get dinner ready. Gotta go.

Being read to is *luxury*! We have lots of talking books. When life is grim (like Mum saying she's never going to wash or iron our clothes anymore, *we* have to do it) I listen to *Just William* read by Martin Jarvis. That cheers me up. Gotta go.

About the gut-spilling sea urchin – I was wrong – it's a gut-spilling sea *cucumber*. It's a pale-skinned fleshy bladder and its defence mechanism is to throw up its guts. We saw a dead one on the beach. Apparently after it's thrown up its guts and totally put the predator right off its meal, it can grow new guts MUST PUT THE POTATOES ON THE STOVE!!!!!!!!!!!

H

Well, there you are. Yesterday I was kind of disappointed when there was no new email in my inbox.

Thanks for the great options.

United Nations sounds good. They fail pretty often.

No news on the money front. Knut has a big job to do - a lot of bookshelves for somebody's new flat. First good contract for quite a while. So he'll be off my back.

I am worn out. Just come back from soccer training. Bad news, too. My days as goalkeeper are over all right.

The tall guy will be our new goalkeeper. Everybody is happy, because we had lost our last match by one goal — and everybody thinks it was my fault because I am too short. But that was not the reason I missed the ball. It was Lukas' fault. The ball came towards me, I was ready to catch it and yelled to Lukas: "LEO! I've got it!" (Not my name, Henni. In soccer, LEO means "Leave it alone. I'll get it.") But that stupid Lukas made a go, touched the ball slightly so it changed direction and I flew past it. Lukas said he didn't, but he lied.

So today our trainer said: "Leo, I know you have a left foot and your right foot isn't bad either. I would rather have you play midfield on the left side. You go down to the line and then

40

center the ball, where your buddy Mustafa is waiting. How's that?"

Well, better than second goalkeeper. Maybe it's not so bad to play on the field. Winter is coming up. In the goal you can get pretty cold.

I found this little comic strip in our newspaper. See, I am not the only one who has the notion of upside-down thinking of Australia.

Papagei.tiff

DÜHÉ

O.AN AUSTRALICUS. YEAH. THEY. NEED A WHILE TILL THEY REALIZE THAT NOW IS DOWN WHAT USED TO BE UP.

Panel 1:

ICH WILL DIESEN BLÖDEN PAPAGEI HIER UMTAUSCHEN!

I WANT TO EXCHANGE THIS STUPID PARROT.

Panel 2:

EIGHT WEEKS?!

AH - EIN "AUSTRALICUS"! JA, DIE BRAUCHEN EIN WEILCHEN, BIS SIE MERKEN, DASS OBEN JETZT UNTEN IST.

ACHT WOCHEN?!

SIE MÜSSEN IHN TRAINIEREN!

YOU HAVE TO TRAIN HIM.

Panel 3:

AND HOW?

UND WIE?

by ©TOM

At the moment I feel a bit like the cat on the
last picture: in the grip.

You don't sound too happy either. Sorry, I can't
come up with an advice. Don't know much about
girls. They stick to themselves. Or go after the
boys from 9th Grade. And my best friend Lina — who
I could ask - moved away two years ago. We grew
up together, we were in the same day care, same
class. Then her mother got a job at the other
end of Germany. Problem is, I am not good at the
telefone and she is definitely not an emailing
person. But when we meet, it's as if she's never
been away.

But your project does sound interesting to me.
Why do people leave home and go as far as
Australia? I don't suppose the Schmidts flew
then, do you? Anyway, if you need any help from
my part, let me know. Bettina is interested in
history and she has a friend who is a historian.

YES: My mother's name is Bettina, and my Dad
is a carpenter. You're right, it sounds as if
somebody made this up. In a book I would think
this is just too obvious. But as my Omi (Grandma)
says: "Das Leben ist eine Wundertüte — Life is a
Miracle Bag. You never know what's in it."

Okay, got to go. Stay in touch.

Yours, hanging his head. Leo

Oh, I almost forgot what I wanted to tell you.

43

Felix.

Today at lunchtime he cared to sit and eat
with me. Then he told me, Sunday after next is a
chess tournament, if I would go with him?

"Sure," I said. I have done this before, as
a kind of mental support. Then Felix asked if
I could get Bettina to drive us to the chess
tournament.

"Drive us?" I said. "Are you kidding? You
know Bettina never uses the car, unless it is
absolutely necessary. Is the tournament out of
town?"

"No, no, it's in Lichtenberg."

"Okay, then we can easily take the train."

"Hey, get real!" he said, kind of cross. "Look
at me."

And only then I realized what bothered him.
Lichtenberg is a district of Berlin where he
might get into trouble.

"You're right," I said. "But why can't your
mother drive us?"

"Forget it," he snapped. He took his tray and
left me there, mouth open.

I wish he would tell me what's bugging him.
    L

DID YOU HAVE THAT *CONVERSE*ATION?

What did Maik say?

And I don't understand. Why can't Felix catch the train? Is he crippled or something?

Because of you I watched soccer on SBS. Nobody scored. I thought there would be 20000 heart attacks if *something* didn't happen, or if it *did!!* Then Hungary got a goal, *phew!* because Danielle (Hungary) was about to bash me up (Paraguay). I like it when they do a little protecting dance around the ball. I bet soccer players are good dancers. When you headbutt the ball, don't you get brain damage?

Australia has its own football game – Aussie Rules, invented in Melbourne, but now it's national. The ball is oval and bounces anyoldhow. It's fast and thrilling – scrambling, leaping, collisions, broken bones.

Thanks for offering to help me find out about the 1915 Schmidts but my project doesn't seem to be going in that direction. Yesterday at lunchtime Athena said, while looking deep into her salad roll, 'Do you still want to do the project with me? I want to do Shetland ponies. My uncle has stables and we could go and stay with them. Do you want to do that?'

I said, 'Yes, I'd love to.'

Then she wiped the corners of her mouth with her little finger but she missed the beetroot on her top lip.

'Okay, Henni,' she said slowly, which made me feel she wasn't sure about asking me.

Shetland *ponies*!

The only time I met a Shetland pony was at the Melbourne

45

Show when I was six – this dumpy shaggy grump in the animal nursery. I guess it had been patted all day by thousands of sticky little hands but my pat was the pat that broke the camel's back. It flashed its eyes and tried to nip me. The attendant leapt over and dragged it away. Shetland ponies . . . oh well . . .

Wish I could do my project with you and Bettina and her historian friend.

No, the Schmidts didn't fly here, they would have come by ship. It was the time of the first plane flights, you know – round the world in 200 days. What port would the Schmidts leave Germany from? I've just looked in the atlas. You don't have much coast.

Kids are teaming up for the project. Jonno and Neil are doing The Sherman Tank – happy as hyenas with machine guns – and going to stay with Neil's cousin in Canberra to visit the War Memorial. (You have to have an 'Approved Host'. Neil says his cousin just got out of the slammer, but Miss Dakin doesn't know that.)

Dad thinks the project is a dumb idea: 'Who wants a couple of demanding kids coming up to Christmas!'

Homework then home work. Who cleans the bathroom at your place?

I'm hanging out for September holidays. One more day. Might be going away.

Still haven't found the two dots. Your cartoon was the best thing about yesterday. I love the look on the cat's face!!!

In the grip too

H

GUESS WHAT!

Yes — your first guess is right.

There is a beautiful once crisp but now a bit smudged 50 Euro bill right beside me on my desk.

Why smudged? By Maik's sticky fingers — the thief's fingers?

Wrong! Maik got the new Converse because — hold on! — he needed them. Simple as that. His old sneakers had been stolen in the gym. At least, that's what he had told his parents. What he didn't say was that one of the boys from 9th Grade had teased him about his "baby" Mickey Mouse sneakers. Felix threw in this bit of information — he always knows what's going on. We should have a gossip paper in school, chief editor: Felix.

When I came home from the soccer match this afternoon, Bettina asked me: "Can you imagine how Lotte could get hold of a 50 Euro bill?"

Well, I could. And you too, I bet.

This is what happened:

That day, when I had put the bill into the envelope, Lotte drew a picture on the envelope — I told you that, didn't I? — a picture of a beggar she had just seen in the street. First she thought it must be fun to sit in the street with a little bowl to collect money from the people passing by. But then Bettina explained that the man was poor. Poor meaning to have not enough money to buy food, never mind ice-cream and stuff. This was shocking for Lotte, because the day before she had got a lecture by Knut.

Lotte had wanted her spaghetti "naked", just with olive oil and salt, no sauce, no salad, nothing green. And Knut saw red! When it comes to food he is not the calm reasonable man anymore. No, he didn't explode, his voice just got real quiet and sharp.

"Nothing green! How stupid! Are you copying the kids in kindergarten? Your body needs vegetables!"

Then he sat down beside her. "Listen, Lotte, not all kids in the world are so lucky that they may choose what they want to eat. Some get only rice and beans, every day. Some get only one small meal a day. And some stay hungry."

"But it's just a few children, isn't it, Knut?"

"More than we would like to imagine."

Knut didn't insist anymore, and Lotte ate her spaghetti the way she wanted to.

Lotte must have taken the 50 Euro while I was busy with my computer. When she had finished her picture, I put the envelope away without checking. She never takes anything without asking. She must have thought this was an emergency.

And she kept the money hidden till next time Bettina took her to the market. She stepped up to the beggar but it took a while till she had the bill out of her pocket, with her chocolate-sticky fingers. So Bettina stopped her. Then she had to give her a 5 Euro bill instead, because Lotte was ready to burst out into a real fit.

It happened this morning while I was at Mustafa's place. Bettina couldn't imagine where Lotte had got the money.

Finally I could tell Bettina the whole story about Maik and my suspicion. I felt like a lot of stones had fallen off my chest — I have heard this expression quite often, but never knew the feeling. Maybe this was the first time ever that I had kept something secret from my parents.

And this is not the only good thing that happened. At today's match I played for the first time in the field! And I scored the winning goal! The opposite goalkeeper was good but I outsmarted him! Well, by pure chance, but it was nice anyway. Mustafa passed the ball, I took it and ran down almost to the line, saw Mustafa in front of the goal, went to center the ball — and kicked a goal! The ball passed the goalkeeper, who was securing the short corner, hit the far post and jumped into the goal! So we won 4:3!

1:0 is a very frequent result in First League matches. We always want to score goals, which drives our trainer mad. He yells: "Go back into defence! Get the ball back!" But most forwards just wait till somebody else passes it to them up front.

A Kopfball — a header — is not too difficult. The point is to brace yourself so it's not your

head that gets hit, but it's your head that pushes
the ball — in the direction you decide, that is
difficult! The best is a Flugkopfball — a flight-
header — this is when a rather low ball is a bit
ahead of you, you jump and fly towards it, body
almost horizontal in the air! Boy, those goals are
beautiful! But in the field, when the ball comes
fast or from high up, I duck, because it does
hurt! Then I rather try to stop it with my chest
or pick it with my foot like a ripe apple ...

Henni, Shetlands might not be so bad. You are
going to be away a while, so it's good to be with
someone you like.

I only got to ride once, a whole day out in the
country. It was great fun, until the horse bent
its head and I shot into the air. But it was on
grass and the horse was a pony, so I didn't hurt
myself. I just got back on. I loved the smell of
the horse's fur. And the swinging of the horse's
body. I felt strong and attached. Maybe that's
what makes people strong — to feel attached?

Bettina just popped in and said: "Are you writing
to that girl? (kind of stressing the word "girl")
Tell her that the passenger ships left from
Hamburg or Bremerhaven. Those to Australia mostly
from Bremerhaven."

Well, you probably won't need that info now.
Will you be able to write when you are on

holidays? Will you go away? Lucky you! I have to wait another two weeks till our holidays come up. We won't go away. Parents have to work. Maybe we spend a few days at the Datsche.

And I have to clean the bathroom. There is a plan, I have to do my share. But as Bettina says, a plan is a plan and life is life. I don't really care to do it. But it's only twice a month.

Okay, I'll close now. There is a late movie on TV, an old one, "Kick it like Beckham". Did they show this in Australia?

Yours very happy hoping that your life will have a happy turn too — Leo

P.S. Ach ja, Felix has black skin. For some people that marks him as someone who doesn't belong, although he was born here like I was, and his mother (black too) also grew up in Germany. In some areas people who are black get treated badly — bad words, spit at, beaten up. Some have even died from such attacks. This is really serious. But I am not always aware of it as Felix must be. He stays clear of certain parts of town. Zum Kotzen ist das! (Makes me sick!)

Lotte!

She's a midget Robin Hood!

When I read about Lotte I snorted so loudly Danielle came rushing in. 'What's so funny?'

I told her.

Danielle goes, '*Yay, little sisters!*'

Phew!! Imagine if you'd accused Maik!!! (And I spent Maths on Friday trying to think of a way of tricking him into admitting it!)

I have news too. Could be good, could be bad.

Remember the house in Cauldron Bay, where Sascha found my note? Well, the owner is *selling* the house!

Ah, that house. No electricity. We slept under mosquito nets on the verandah. And it's near the most beautiful beach in the world. Danielle says I'm a worrywart but this is definitely a God moment for me.

Dear God,

Please look after the Schmidts' house and let good people buy it – a family, like a breath of new life.

Tibor, Zev's dad, told me it was being sold. Tibor has asked Mr Barnett, the owner, about some old tools under the house and Mr B said, 'If you want 'em you better go and get 'em.'

'What about the boxes of books?' I asked Tibor.

Tibor said, 'Ask him.'

So in the moment of boldness I'm going to have this evening, I'll phone Mr B and ask for the books. You can tell so

52

much about people from their books. Mr B might think they're worth a lot of money. He might want me to buy them.

Otherwise IT IS GLORIOUS GLORIOUS HOLIDAYS, even if Mum gave a lecture this morning – 'How to Use the Washing Machine'.

Hey, I totally forgot !   *Yay* for the winning goal! GoSoccerman!

That film was called *Bend it like Beckham* here. I haven't seen it, but I will now I'm more into soccer.

Danielle and I are going to stay with an old friend of Mum's. Mum and Dad are getting rid of us – they are both flat out at work. But it's okay. I'm taking a stack of books and Danielle is taking her tennis racquet. She'll find a brick wall. She always does. Don't know if I'll be able to email or when we're coming home.

Thanks, Bettina, for the information about passenger ships and Bremerhaven.

Why would a family from Germany go to Cauldron Bay where they didn't know anybody? You don't just *happen* to go to a lonely place like that. You go there on *purpose*. And Konrad Schmidt's house will last for centuries – yet they left Cauldron Bay in a hurry. I'm sure they intended to return. What went wrong?

Athena said, 'I bought you a book on Shetlands. They're like living soft toys.'

I said, 'Stumpy little cave horses.'

She gave me a funny look through her hair. Ah, *that's* why she likes Shetlands. She's like one herself!

Archie and Arvi are doing their project on conscription and staying with Archie's grandpa who was sent to Vietnam. Archie is the other brain in our class, but he's sort of the opposite to me. He's small, noisy, chews continuously, reads graphic novels and cracks pathetic jokes. (I crack hilarious ones!)

I asked Archie if there was conscription for the First World War.

'Dunno,' goes Archie. 'I'll find out for you.'

I was telling Mum about it when Danielle came in.

'What's conscription?' asks Danielle.

'Conscription is when you have to do military training,' I said. 'To join the army. Compulsory. No choice.'

Now Conscription is Danielle's new word. Last night she did a volcanic eruption.

Danielle: Out of *all my friends* this is the only house with cooking conscription!

Mum: Don't you want to be independent? Wouldn't you like to be able to prepare delicious meals for your friends?

Danielle: *NO!*

Well that's it for now, Dinosaurusofcommunication. When I get back the first thing I will do is check my inbox.

Wish me luck for the phone call about the books.

Tschüs   I found the dots!

And lots of other things! ☀ "(⊡ ☆☆☆ ☺ 🐒🐾🔍 ❹

    H

MONTAG, 19.SEPTEMBER

Homework done — French vocabulary for a test
tomorrow. I make up my own test in the computer
and practice the spelling — I am not very good
at spelling. My emails are fine because I use the
spelling check. Too bad we can't use it in the
classroom. My grades would be much better.

I know you are away and having a good time,
but I thought I would just start a letter and
keep it going like a diary.

Conscription! Maybe your Konrad Schmidt left
Germany to get away from conscription. Like my
Dad, who left his home town and went to Berlin
to avoid military service. That was before the
wall came down. West Berlin had no army, no
conscription — but that changed in 1990 when East
Germany (German Democratic Republic) became part
of West Germany (Federal Republic of Germany).
The army immediately tried to conscript the
ones who had escaped to Berlin. They went after
Knut too, but he managed to get out of military
service. He didn't answer the mails they sent.
And he was not at home when they came for him.
First by chance, then he moved to live for a
while with friends. That's where he met Bettina,
by the way. When Knut turned twenty-five, the
"battle" was over.

55

I don't want to be a soldier. No way. But it's
still many years till military service. Maybe by
that time Germany will have completely done away
with the army! (Like Costa Rica!)

Nice dream.

Bettina just called for dinner. *Save as* ...

MITTWOCH, 21.SEPTEMBER

Thick air over here (meaning trouble's brewing).

Last night was parents' night at school. And
there Bettina had learned something I hadn't told
her. Because I was ashamed.

Still am. Shall I tell it?

Rather not. You will stop writing.

No, you won't.

Okay.

Now. (I can still *delete*.)

All right. Remember Maik? It's about him and
other guys. And me.

It started in Math. The teacher was talking
over the heads of most of us, scribbling away on
the blackboard. Maik was clowning around, mostly
with Marika. The teacher finally got mad and told
Maik he will inform his parents. Then Maik said
with a squeaky voice: "Please, don't, they'll
spank me!" rolling his eyes and raising his arms
like a little child, so everybody laughed. Well,
I think he was serious, since his foster parents
already cut his allowance and let him watch TV

only on weekends because he had flunked the Math
test. But the teacher got mad and told Maik, one
more word and he'll get one hour detention. Maik
protested again — why only him and not Marika?
Lately he had tried to behave, because he was
told he could not go on our ski-trip in January
if there was one more incident. There wasn't.
Because the bell rang.

Most of us raced out of the classroom,
relieved. And outside we played catch. We
were running, pushing, touching, screaming,
laughing. Loud, we were loud, fast, and things
got tough. There was something that was more
than just a game. It got kind of serious. I felt
uncomfortable and stood aside, watching. First it
had been boys and girls, real fun. Then all of a
sudden it was boys chase girls, try to touch them
not just on the shoulders. Then it was only boys
and Marika. Then it was mostly Maik and Marika.
And all of a sudden he had her in a corner, with
a group of six, seven boys around, and me too.
They kind of drew me, don't know why. I am just
watching, I remember thinking.

Then I heard Marika screaming: "Get your
dirty hands off!" Maik laughed and somebody held
Marika, and Maik lifted her skirt. And I was
there with the others, staring — the yelling of
the boys in my ear. They cheered like they
were about to shoot a goal. And Marika trying
to defend herself and Maik at her skirt, and
me still not saying anything, just staring like

a rabbit in front of a snake. My heart went 200 beats a minute.

Then Mustafa came.

He checked the situation in a moment. He yelled: "Stop it! Are you crazy! What do you think you are doing!" And in that moment everybody kind of put on the brakes. Maik had an awkward grin in his face, saying: "Hey, this is just fun!" Marika yelled: "You liar! You damn liar!" And she pushed her way through the group. She had tears in her eyes.

That moment our home-room teacher came — this is how the whole story got to be told on parents' night.

Maik might get thrown from school.

Everybody involved will have to stay after school and write a report. Why we did it, and how we felt. Felix was lucky because he had stayed in the classroom, still busy with the Math problem nobody else had been interested in. I didn't ask him what he would have done.

In class we had learned about the first boycott day against Jewish stores, shortly after the Nazis had gained power in 1933. I had thought, no, I would have never been part of any of this. Now I think I might have been one of those spectators. But if you stand and look on, you sort of encourage the ones who act — you are what humus is for a plant.

Bettina was really mad. That doesn't mean she yells or anything like that. She just gets this dark glow in her eyes, then she takes a deep breath and starts her lecture.

"All atrocities start somewhere where it doesn't seem to be important," she said. "Just looking under a girl's skirt is no rape, right? But this is where rape begins. And I don't know what is worse, acting or watching. Maybe Maik wouldn't have done anything if the others wouldn't have watched him."

Meaning me.

I felt so bad.

Why didn't I do what Mustafa did?

Bettina said it was my lack of experience.

"Remember Mustafa in the underground?" she said.

I do. We were going someplace — Mustafa, Bettina, Lotte and me — by train. There was a man sitting opposite to us, dressed like a gentleman, but drunk. He stared at Mustafa and muttered something like the invasion of the Turks, Germany to the Germans, things like that. Real ugly, real mean. Bettina got uneasy and drew Lotte closer, but before she could say anything, Mustafa stood up. He put himself in front of that guy, legs wide apart to stand the rocking of the train, and said: "You shut up or I'll shut you up!" The man stared at him, open-mouthed, then snapped: "You shut up, you Kanaka. Go home!"

The train brakes screamed as the train pulled into the station. Bettina shoved Lotte over to me, ready to get up and do something if necessary. I saw how Mustafa was trembling but he didn't back away. Instead he said: "My home is here. YOU get out of this train, or do you want me to make you?" He raised his fists and the guy scrambled to his feet. He gave Mustafa a killing look and stumbled out — swearing like hell once he had hit the station platform.

Mustafa said he is sick of being pissed off and he is not going to take it, even if it means to get beaten up. He never was, though. By the way, the other passengers clapped when the guy had left.

Does experience mean you have to know how it feels to be picked on? Has my life been too sunny?

And the worst thing is, I couldn't attend soccer training tonight, because Knut had to go back to work and Bettina had a meeting right after work. So I had to stay with Lotte.

GRRRR.

SONNABEND, 24.SEPTEMBER
Didn't want to write anymore. Didn't want to send what I've written. I had it deleted twice, but saved it from the trash.

No soccer match for me today.

I did not play because I hadn't shown up for the training last Wednesday. Of the kids who come to the training, fourteen get invited for the match on Saturday. That's the rule.

After the match the trainer called me — sorry,

very sorry. Bettina's excuse for Wednesday had
got lost. So it hadn't been my fault. AND they
had missed me! Mustafa had been alone in the
center without my passes.

Still don't know if I want to mail this.
Why should you want to read all that stuff?

I read your last letter again.

Okay. I'll send it.

SONNTAG, 25.SEPTEMBER

A day later. I didn't send it.

But now I will.

HENNI, I just have to tell you: **I have seen
Cauldron Bay!**

The Schmidts' Haus! Boy, how it is sitting
between the gum trees, with the stone steps at
the side! I tried to imagine you there. A lizard
slipped by. A parrot sat on the roof looking down
to the porch as if he was checking the visitors!
I saw the dark area underneath the house, but the
camera didn't go into it. And the woman (who is
shaped like a light bulb) in front of the store!
The tea-trees, the dunes, the white sandy beach,
the blue sea, the surfers! Wow! Never in my life
have I seen anything that beautiful, in real,
I mean. Not to mention spending vacations there!

NO — it wasn't telepathy — it was Sascha's
DVD. Remember Sascha, my uncle, the cameraman and
note-finder? After he had given me the note, he
and Tania had left again, but now they are done

61

with all their filming and researching. And last night they came to see us.

First thing Sascha asked me: "Did you write to that Australian girl?" And I said: "Yes, I did, in fact, we are still writing." Then he gave me this knowing smirk, so I said: "Stop your dirty thoughts, we are just friends!" — "Hey, hey," he said, "nothing dirty about what you think what I think! Wanna see pictures?"

Of course I wanted!

And then he showed me — first Cauldron Bay, their private shots. Tania likes to document with her camcord where they were, where they worked. Then images from surfing, also historical material — from the Hawaiian kings of past centuries to the beach kings of today, the riders of the big waves. You wouldn't believe what I saw! Gigantic waves — and they dare to ride them. One surfer said: "We think we chase the waves, but actually it's the waves that chase us." To ride the real big ones they get out with little motorboats, like motorbikes on water — incredible.

When the surfers lose balance, they get swallowed by white foam — and luckily spit out later, bruised, half suffocated. I would never ever do it! Though Sascha said: "It seems to be the ultimate kick. Surfers get depressed when there are no waves."

Well, I still feel a little bad about this mail.

Sascha asked me to take care of their flat, water the plants, because they have to go away again for ten days or so, and the friend they are living with will be out of town too.

So somebody still trusts me.

Do you?

L

Okay, I'll tell the truth too.

I held my breath reading about Maik going at Marika. My eyes skipped down the page, scared of what I might read but wanting to know. I was like you, frozen, except *reading*! – but also **angry**!!!

I thought *Maik!* You *sleazy filthy* **RAT!**

Where are the girls? Stick *together!*

Thank *God* for you, Mustafa!

And now what, Maik? You don't fix that by just saying Sorry.

Danielle would have kicked him in the nuts. Shit happens fast but she's quick.

And what would I have done? I don't know. Probably nothing, like you, Leo – an innocent bystander? Bettina's right, innocent but guilty. Or you stop being you and become a member of a side. I think our lives *are* too sunny to know how we would respond. We haven't been put to the test.

I saw something like that too. Krystelle Ball – honestly, that's her name! – is a fast and flirty wing defence in netball. Well, Hayden in Year 9 thinks every girl on earth lusts after him, and when Krystelle grabbed his cap and ran off with it, Hayden and his mates went after her like wolves. They chased her across the oval and out of the school grounds. She dropped the cap, but they still chased her up the hill until they were tiny figures running on the road, on the footpath, the road, footpath, road, dodging cars. Kids were screaming and barracking, but I was afraid, thinking, What will they do if they catch her?

Hayden and his pack wandered back. She out-ran them. The End.

Except someone wrote a foul sort of threat about her in the underpass near the station. They spelt OR ELSE as OR ELCE. I did nothing about that either. But someone painted it out.

Trouble is, while you're watching it, the bad stuff speeds up until it's going too fast to stop.

How is Marika?

If Maik gets chucked out he'll go to a new school and what's that going to solve? He'll be the weird new foster-child kid again. Probably make him worse. But the teacher wasn't fair. Marika wasn't threatened with detention too, and you said Maik had been behaving better. What did you say in that report thing you had to write?

I don't want to think about it anymore. I'm changing the subject to something more pleasant. Yeah. That happens too.

Isn't Cauldron Bay beautiful?

It's so extraordinary that you know it, in Berlin, but nobody here does. On a school excursion to a city beach, the teacher said, 'Isn't it glorious?' There were cigarette butts and the sand was churned up and the waves were pathetic and I thought, No, it's crummy. You should see Cauldron.

How did the surfies feel about Cauldron being filmed? Bet Sascha did some fast talking.

They're mad, those guys. In one of the surfing magazines they have a photo: 'Injury of the Month.'

I'm longing for Cauldron Bay, especially as this holiday is such a non-event ☺ Well, it wasn't *so* bad for me, I read five books, but Danielle was going round the twist.

Dad collected us early this morning, a bit late to get Danielle to a tennis game. Dad's her coach. We cannoned along

D's NEW serve.jpg

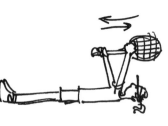
Salute the Net

The Long Wait

WHACK.

the freeway . . . talking of cannons, Danielle has invented a new serve.

Danielle + new serve working = certain victory

Danielle + new serve not working = certain defeat

Dad says stick with the old serve, but Danielle says she can't do the old serve anymore, the new one mucked it up.

Dad says try and tone it down a bit, but Danielle says if it doesn't have the power it doesn't work.

We arrive at the court and Danielle's serve was in the groove. *Pow!* Ace! *Pow!* Ace! Fan*tas*tic! Then she broke a string. She borrowed a racquet.

Whack!   To Africa!

      Whack!   Finland!

            Whack!   Tasmania!

Dad was groaning. Then to make light of wild shots she did a little dance, then it all went downhill fast in a very Danielle way.

Driving home she continued the who-cares act. Dad was black as thunder, didn't say a word, but once we were in the house he *roared*, 'You were just being *stupid* out there. You weren't even *trying*! You threw the whole thing away.'

Mum cut in. 'Martin, it's only a *game* for heaven's sake.'

But Dad raged on. 'She made a fool of herself.' He switched to Danielle. 'You insult your opponent playing like that. You insult the umpire. You insult your supporters.' He switched to Mum. 'She's a clown. She hasn't got it. She gave up.'

'*She* says, "Stuff *you!*"' yelled Danielle, and slammed out.

Dad snapped. 'I'm going in to work, I have a presentation on Wednesday and I've totally wasted today.'

There were a couple of thumps on the roof but we didn't take any notice.

'What?' goes Mum, angry because Dad has begun working at weekends.

While they were yelling at each other, I went to find Danielle. She's been Dad's Golden Girl and it must have felt awful when her serve went kaput with everyone watching. She was sitting on her bed smouldering under her eyebrows, shredding her sweatband.

'Don't speak!' she snapped.

Out the window I saw Dad getting into the car. A flash of purple caught my eye.

'Dad! *STOP!*' I screamed.

He couldn't hear me and started the car, but Mum heard the panic in my voice. 'Martin, *STOP!*'

Chocked under the rear tyre was Danielle's Wilson N code 26 racquet – with nanotechnology and the purple grip that she had wanted for so long. Danielle had wedged it in so Dad would back over it.

Well, the shit hit the fan all over again. She'd flung her tennis shoes onto the roof and whacked balls all over the neighbourhood. Mum pushed Dad into the car and they drove off.

Now, Danielle is gutsing down chocolate ice-cream, seething about Dad's total unfairness . . . and she's *never* going to play tennis again. I am sitting here having a first-class worry.

Much later.

Mum came back in a bad mood. Finally Dad came home in a taxi. Apologies all round. Very sorry Danielle. Very sorry Dad. Won't happen again. Sorry. Sorry. Love you very much.

Love you too, etc etc No mention of tennis.

I'm glad I could tell you. I don't feel so stirred up anymore.
Now I might even be able to sleep.

Tschüs Soccerman.

See you at the World Premiere   of Sascha's film,
                    on the   Big   Screen,
          with
                 Profound Surround
                      Sound,
                          middle

          seat,
                         front
                              row.

                                        H

Henni loves you.
Do you love her?
You are Henni's boyfriend.
She prints out all your letters
and pits them in a box.
She is always talking about you.
The first thingmy sister does
after school is check her emails.

I'M GETTING THE BOOKS FROM CAULDRON BAY!!!!!!
    It was easy!
    Mr Barnett, the owner, is generous and very chatty.
He's sad they're selling the house but the family says it's too far
to go. He asked me if I wanted to buy it and I said, 'Yes, if it's no
more than $27.40.'
    I asked him about the Schmidts and he reckoned there was
something mysterious going on there too. 'More than meets the
eye,' he said.
    On the title of the land the Schmidts' address was near
Horsham, which is a town in the Wimmera, a farming area
north-west of Melbourne. They must have lived there before
Cauldron Bay.

Wouldn't it be extraordinary to meet (*Drrrrrrrrrrum roll!*) – THE
LIVING LINK – descendants of the Schmidts? They would know
why the family left so suddenly.
    Hey, *they* should buy the house!
    I'm going to Cauldron Bay with Tibor, not this weekend but
next, to collect the stuff.
    Home work. Uggh!
    Read you
    Henni

What's going on?

I've emailed you twice.

It's your turn.

Did I say something wrong?

I'm sorry if I did. I was trying to be honest.

We've talked about difficult things. Maybe I'm not using the right words. Maybe I don't *know* the right words. Maybe I don't know myself. Was it something I said about Maik and Marika?

It felt like we were both being open and honest and funny.

Please tell me if I have done something wrong, Leo.

Henni

I'm going to Cauldron Bay with Tibor this weekend.

Melbourne, Thursday 6 October 5.45pm

???? ??????

?????? ???? ????? ? ? ??????? ? ? ??? ? ??????? ???
?????   ???????? ???? ???????? ???? ????? ???? ??????
???? ???? ?? ?? ? ???????? ??????   ?????? ? ???
????? ??
????? ??? ?????? ?? ?????? ?????? ????
???? ???????? ??? ??? ????????? ????????????

???? ????

?

???
Ask your sister!

Been away a few days, in our Datsche. Felix didn't come. He said he had to stay home, then he looked away. Something with your parents? I asked. No, no everything okay, he said. It's just ... then he stopped and started to talk about the chess tournament.

Mustafa had to help in the grocery store to substitute for his sister. She is preparing for an exam.

Antek's band is allowed to play in school two hours a day. He wasn't going to miss one session. He told his parents he is practicing for the school concert in December. Classical guitar. Ha!

Holidays were boring. The weather was miserable. But I caught a big fish. Fed us all.

Leo

P.S. Maik was not thrown from school. There was a long talk between our home-room teacher, Maik and Marika. Maik apologized and she accepted it. Maik has to switch to the G/A course in Math, which is an easier level. AND he is banned from our ski-trip in January. His comment: "Pah! Who wants to break their legs anyway!"

Hmm. His face spoke differently.

I can't see how this punishment makes Maik
change. He just ducks.

He's not the only one who can't come. Two
kids said their parents don't have the money.
One girl says her father doesn't want her to go.
But it's still three months. Any soccer match
can be decided in the last minute ...

Melbourne, Sunday 9 October 8pm

IT'S ALL RIGHT. I'VE KILLED HER!

Pity you can only kill someone once!!!

That was so embarrassing. I went beetroot from the top of my head to the ends of my toes, and I'm *tall*. What can I say? I'm truly truly sorry, Leo.

Unfortunately I can't say it will never happen again because with Danielle you can't be sure of anything.

Tibor and I just got back from Cauldron Bay. We drove there yesterday, then back today.

JeepersLeo, it's a   L   O   N   G   way!

We stayed in the house, well not so much *in* as *at*. Camped on the verandah. The birds woke me early. Tibor slept on. He would have slept through a bomb he was so tired. I went for a walk. When I reached the top of the dunes I felt the same thrill that I felt the first time I saw the bay. The sea is so mighty and huge and alive.

I told Leopold his relatives should buy the house.

I have Maths, History and Indonesian homework and I'm very tired. How can sitting in a car for hours and hours make you feel so beat?

The boxes of books are here at my feet – precious treasure! Soon I'll be getting to know the Schmidts. I had a quick peek. I'll need a translator that's for sure. Talking of German . . . how do you say 'Knut'? It's such a funny name. I can't imagine calling my father Nut. In English, nuts is another name for balls!?!?

Another slice of Danielle for you. My parents are fighting their

own battles at work right now, and tonight I complained.
'It feels like Danielle and I have to raise ourselves this year.'

Quick as a flash Danielle goes, 'In that case, I'm saying there's a 500 times raise in pocket money.'

Okay, homework.

I do talk about you a lot.
    But I'm not going to un-kill her.
    H

Hi Henni — glad you crushed Danielle. I hate this love stuff, like, when you talk to a girl there must be something behind it. As if guys can't think of anything else. Or girls, in that case. Stupid Danielle. I really freaked for a moment.

I don't really know what love is about.

Okay, I love my parents and my little sister. But that is different.

I do know that it is nice to touch someone and to be touched. When Mustafa and I wrestle for fun, it feels good. We embrace when we meet. Most Turkish boys do that. Men too. I would never put my arm on Maik's shoulder — he would jump and tell me he is not gay. But with Mustafa — no problem.

You know what?

Yesterday my voice cracked. Out of the blue. I said something to Lotte, like, pass the rice please, and that "bitte" came from deep down I don't know where.

Bettina laughed, Knut grinned. And I coughed and cleared my throat, as if I had choked. Lotte passed the rice and said: "Are you going to be a singer, Leo?"

So much to sisters!

Speaking of Knut — of course y o u would pronounce it nut! My Dad is no nut but sure has balls! In German you pronounce the K and our "u" is pronounced like "oo".

Say it: K-noot!

Okay.

Try Knabe (old fashioned for boy)

Or Knacki (a prisoner) — that would be like K-nuckee for you

Or Knackarsch

No, that's rude, sorry.

Boy, when I read about the row in your family, I thought that was scary, although I liked the sorry bit afterwards. With us, there is no yelling, no explosion. When Knut is mad he gets even quieter than usual. Then you get a comment that hits right into your center and you feel like somebody has pulled the carpet you have been standing on.

Sometimes I feel like yelling out loud.

I keep thinking about something that happened in school. We were sitting in the cafeteria and we had a discussion about order and rules and stuff. Well, actually me and Antek, because Felix just ate and didn't join. Antek said: "There has to be order, if not, everybody would do what he wants."

Just as he was saying that, a teacher passed our table. She teaches Ethics and Philosophy in the upper grades. She stopped and said: "And what's wrong with that? Shouldn't everybody be free to do what he or she wants?"

Antek stared at her and said: "This creates complete chaos!"

The teacher laughed. "Think about it!" she said, and left.

Antek shook his head.

Felix's eyes grew big and he said: "Yeah, she's right."

Me: "Boy, I don't know. Have to think about it."

Not now, though.

I'll be away for a few days, visiting Omi, Knut's mother. She lives in a small town just north of Frankfurt. Bettina drives us there — me and Lotte — and then goes back. Omi has a swimming pool in the basement of her house. Opa built it with a friend. Opa died last year. He was a plumber and a bricklayer and could do just about everything with his hands. Like Knut.

I turned out to be a person with no special skills. Only my feet seem to work fine!

I will be back next Sunday, and yes, I will be happy to do some translations for you. Whatever you might find. The house in Cauldron Bay looked great. I would buy it too. And the whole bay with it. Is it possible to own a bay? Is it possible to own the sea?

Okay, got to go. Gina (my other grandmother, Bettina's mother) just arrived for afternoon tea. There is going to be cake with it! Käsekuchen! Cheesecake. Fluffy, sweet, creamy, great.

See you in a week!

Leo

Hello Knabe! How was your holiday? It was great to get your email!

Feels like we're back to normal and BOY OH BOY DO I HAVE NEWS?   *JA!*

A Schmidt *treasure trove!*

My room is a German history museum. The stuff from the three boxes from Cauldron Bay is spread on my bed, the floor, my desk, chair, everywhere.

There is an old, very worn pair of binoculars.

There are four letters in strange handwriting from Horsham, with an address. (Remember Mr B said the Schmidts had come from Horsham? Could be a vital clue to the Living Link!)

There's a plan of a building – just a pencil sketch – but nicely drawn. Konrad probably did this. One room has the word Werkstaht written on it ? could be Werkstatt? What does that mean? It was folded up inside a huge illustrated encyclopedia.

There's a book (Buch?) about a German woman, Amalie Dietrich, who must have had something to do with Australian wildlife, because it has illustrations of our birds and snakes etc (bird is Vogel?)

A butterfly collection (Schmetterling?)

A sweet little blue bottle about the size of a cotton reel

And Buch! Buch! Buch!!!! about birds, plants, butterflies, nature stuff and building, construction, carpentry etc. One bird book is very worn and has pencil notes all through about bird sightings. I've put it with the binoculars. Boy, they liked Vogels!

And now – my skin tingled when I found this! – *The Victorian Reading Book, Class II*, and written in the front

Leopold Schmidt 1913

Inside I found pressed wildflowers. Then, tucked in an article about Our Motherland, scraps of paper where Leopold had practised his English – *his actual writing*. I'll scan it all for you.

There are also his boys' adventure books, all in English – *Treasure Island*, *Moby-Dick*, *The Adventures of Huckleberry Finn* etc

I found a note by Konrad in the front of the bird book. It might be important – dated, on the back, 15 Januar 1916. I can make out the first line. *My* something *Bettina* something something Sohn Leopold – *son Leopold* ? then two lines down it says the word 'die' – maybe *in case I die*? I'll scan this first. It also has a name, Ting Tang Tellerlein. Ting Tang – a Chinese person?

I was disappointed when nobody in my family wanted to unpack the boxes with me, but now I'm glad. I went through them by myself, finding out about Konrad and Bettina, Gretel, Christa and Leopold. Three hours have gone in a flash.

The earliest date on the letters is 1913. The Schmidts were in Cauldron Bay earlier than we thought. But all the letters are in GERMAN!! May as well be in Martian!

Yikes! Just heard Mum and Dad come home and I'm supposed to have lunch ready!

Translation. Don't forget.

Read you

H

Konrad Note.jpg

Leos READER.jpg

THE
VICTORIAN
READING
❦ BOOK ❦

Meine geliebte Betina, mein lieber Sohn Leopold!

Da ich nicht weiß, was in diesen unsicheren Zeiten auf uns zukommen mag, habe ich die Papiere an einem sicheren Ort deponiert. Für den Fall, daß wir getrennt werden sollten, denkt an
Ting, Tang, Tellerlein!
Dann werdet ihr sie gewiß finden.
Kopf hoch! Wir haben schon Schlimmeres überstanden!
Es umarmt Euch Euer getreuer Ehemann und Vater.
Konrad

ONE SHILLING

OUR MOTHER-LAND.—I.

whole	peo′-ple	pa′-rent	vis′-it
fan′-cy	sup-pose′	ar-rive′	edge
wrap	Lon′-don	pave′-ment	guides
car′-riage	mo′-tor	sing′-le	dif′-fi-cult
Au′-tumn	hedg′-es	fol′-low-ing	dif′-fer-ent

1. Far away across the sea, many thousands of miles from us, there lie some islands, known as the British Isles. The largest is called Great Britain, and in it are the countries of England, Scotland, and Wales. The next in size is Ireland, and there are many little islands besides.

2. The whole of Britain is only about the same size as our own State of Victoria; yet from that little land have gone out the people who have built up the British Empire, of which we are a part.

3. Almost all the people who live in our State are of British blood. Most of the boys and girls who read this book have been born in Victoria; but most of them will find that their parents, or their grand-parents, came from Britain. This is why we call Britain our Mother-land.

Today is the Birthday of the King of England

England is the ~~motherland~~ Mother-land of Australia.

My motherland is Germany I am Australian

My name is Leopold Schmidt.

I like to watch birds and know Australian plants.

My father is a furniture maker. He is making a grand side-board of Black Wood.

Today I see a green hood orchid.

...and dries up the trees and the grass, so that bush fires break out very easily. But, in England, it is a very cold month, and we must wrap ourselves up in thick, warm clothes.

6. About this time of the year, if you stay in London, you may see a fog, and you will not like that at all. A London fog is often so thick, that it is difficult to find your way along the streets. You can stand on the edge of the pavement, and be quite unable to see a house which is so close that you could touch it with a long stick.

7. Everyone has to go very slowly and carefully; and many people lose their way,

Hello?

Anybody home?

You said, 'See you in a week.' The week was up yesterday.

How about the treasure trove!!! I imagined Leopold sitting in the rough wooden make-do school room, carefully arranging the wildflowers to press them, and looking up from his writing to see rosellas in the gum trees. The Schmidts wanted to know about *everything*! Leopold picked up English fast if he could read those novels. I think the Schmidts collected the butterflies themselves. I recognise three varieties. You know, every time I opened a new book I hoped I'd find a photo of the family, but no luck.

Did you get my attachment with the note for translation?

I showed Athena the bird book, Leopold's *Reader*, the little blue bottle and the butterflies to persuade her that history is interesting, but she's fixed on those grumpy Shetlands! (*sigh*) I've read about them. They came from islands at the top of Scotland. Wish they'd stayed there.

I looked up *Knackarsch* in the German dictionary but it didn't have it. Come on – tell me! You can't just say, 'No, that's rude, sorry.'

Dad and Danielle have a truce, and there's a new tube of balls in the bucket in the laundry. The old tube had sixty balls in it before Danielle whacked them into the sky, and now everywhere you go in our suburb, Baker's Hill, you see kids and dogs playing with tennis balls.

I thought about the love stuff . . .

A boy doesn't have to be a boyfriend; he can be a friend who is a boy, like Zev is to me. In Cauldron Bay last Easter, Tara flirted with him, which felt strange . . . and he . . . well there was something going on. Then I started to notice things about Zev, like the corners of his eyes when he smiles and the way he scratches his head. I started to see him in a different way because she liked him.

I had a dream about the Schmidts last night. Konrad lifting Gretel onto the ship's rail to watch the sea birds. Then I was in a city street with horses and carts and those first cars, when someone waved from the back section of one of those cable trams and it was Leopold. We went up into a room, dark with thick curtains and luggage everywhere, lit by a heavy kerosene lamp. The little girls, with big bows in their hair, were playing with china dolls behind some boxes. Then Bettina served up the soup and it was dark red. Leopold whispered in my ear that I didn't have to eat it.

So what does that mean? Reminds me – better get cooking.

Leftover curry for dinner tonight and f l u f f f f f f y rice. I'm the Queen of Fluffy Rice. Zev's mum taught me. And microwave pappadams.

Translation please
    Read you
    soon
    Soccerman

    H

Berlin, Dienstag, 18.Oktober 22.15

SOMETHING HORRIBLE HAS HAPPENED.

I don't have much time.

Bettina has already told me twice to go to bed. There is a History test tomorrow.

As if that matters now.

But I can't tell.

Felix begged me not to tell anyone. And he meant it. Boy, I've never seen anyone so frightened.

But I suppose I can tell you.

You won't be a danger.

Felix has to hide because the police want to deport him and his mother.

Yesterday, early in the morning when he came back from jogging, he saw two policemen lead his mother out of the building where they live and push her into a police car. Felix ducked behind a hedge. When the police car drove off he ran away, scared like hell. He roamed about all day till he managed to meet me after school.

I took him to Sascha's flat. Remember? I am taking care of the place because nobody's there.

So. I have no idea what's going to happen next.

Got to go now. Good night.

Leo

JeepersLeo!

What did Felix's mother *do*?

If she did something wrong he shouldn't have to be deported as well.

WOW! This is scary, especially if the cops find out.

I guess you're going to school. Is anyone helping you hide him?

Where's Felix's father?

Be careful.

H

I feel bad asking, but if you have a second could you translate the note? No, forget it.

Day three.

Nothing's changed.

Felix still hiding, his mother still in jail.

Everybody is worried.

Although all friends know Felix is safe.

Felix asked me to slip a note into his father's mailbox. That was tricky. The entrance door was locked, so I had to wait till somebody came out. Felix did not want me to meet his father. He was afraid that his father would make me to tell him where Felix is and then go to see him. And the police would track him down.

Felix thinks they will not deport his mother as long as they don't have him. Because they also want him out of this country.

Deport him to a country he's never been before. No, not true. They have visited his grandparents in Namibia once, but he doesn't remember it.

Felix doesn't want to get anybody involved because it is illegal to hide him.

But I can do it, because I am not fourteen yet. If you're under fourteen you cannot be charged if you violate a law.

Still I'd rather not think about what might happen if the police find out.

This sounds like a detective story. But it is real, I swear.

90

Felix's mother hasn't committed any crime. Neither has Felix. They were just born at the wrong place at the wrong time. They don't have German citizenship. And something happened with their permit to stay here. So all of a sudden they are considered "illegal" immigrants.

It's hard to understand the whole business. I'll try to explain.

Okay: Felix's mother Nali was born in 1972 in Southern Africa. She lived with her mother in a refugee camp, while her father fought for the liberation of their country, Namibia, which was under South African — apartheid — rule. The refugee camp was attacked and many people died. Little Nali and other children were sent to East Germany, to grow up in peace and to be future fighters for freedom. Years later Nali's parents found asylum in Europe. They got their daughter back from East Germany, and tried to live a normal life in West Germany. For Nali it was difficult. She missed the kids from her boarding school, who had become her family.

When Namibia became liberated, Nali's parents went back, but Nali stayed here. She felt at home in Germany. She had started to study clarinet at the music academy in Berlin. And she had met Mario, Felix's father, who was a student from Peru. (No German citizenship either!)

Nali's home is Germany, but she only had a temporary permit to stay here. After her exam,

91

she got a lot of support to have it extended, because she had a job in an orchestra. This went on for years. She worked for different orchestras, for theaters, had all kinds of engagements, and got her permit (and that for Felix) extended. But this year, they refused to renew it because she has no job. She was told to take her son and go "back" to Namibia. She protested but without success. At the end they arrested her, to fly her and Felix out.

Now I know why Felix behaved so strangely. He had been turned into a stranger.

Felix's parents are not married. There is a reason why, but Felix doesn't know. It's got something to do with citizenship and things like that. But married or not married — how can anybody think of tearing a family apart?

His mother is in some sort of jail where there are many others waiting to be deported.

I never even knew that such jails existed.

It is so disgusting. I mean Felix was born here and goes to school here. This is his HOME!

Yes, I am back to school. Holidays are over. The talk is about Felix and where he could be hiding. Maik thinks this is a big adventure and he wants to be part of it.

Antek says, the law is the law, there is no way around it.

That's so stupid. Antek's family only has German citizenship because they have one German grandfather. The rest of his family has always been Polish, and lived in Poland till they turned German and moved over here ten years ago. Our History teacher is preparing a unit about citizenship and nationalities. That's all I need now.

Mustafa gives me these funny looks, as if he suspects something. I almost told him, then I thought of his cousin Ümit, who is working at the family's foodstore, in the back, preparing delis they are selling. I think he has no valid residence permit. And Mustafa is going to turn fourteen pretty soon. Don't want to draw him into this and cause him trouble.

I feel like I am stuffed to the brim and about to burst.

Right after school I go over to Felix. We watch movies. Sascha has lots of good ones.

Felix has got some money, so I could buy him something to eat. Döner and Currywurst and French fries and loads of chocolate. All kinds of junk. Felix eats as if he is starving.

He is so nervous. Doesn't even want to play chess. Chews on the collar of his shirt, it's all soggy. I think he needs clean clothes.

He doesn't want me to leave when I have to.

My head is spinning, I'm so tired. I'm off.

Well, one for you, Henni: *Knackarsch* is "crack bum". Meaning a very beautiful bum.

Ha ha ha.

Night, Henni. Thanks for listening.
Leo

I don't feel like Leo the lion, not the tiniest
bit. Wish I could tell my parents, but Felix begs
me not to. With glittering eyes.

Melbourne, Thursday 20 October 6pm

JeepersLeo! *Double* jeepers!!!!!!   Felix is *in* a chess game!

He's a little black pawn, and you're the lonely knight protecting him, but you can't tell your queen or king or anyone! And Sascha's the castle but he doesn't know it. And you're playing against the government, who want to wipe him off the board, and *they're making up the rules!!!*

They were happy to have Nali when she was performing, but now they think they can just kick her out! That is *not fair!!!*

Walking home from school, I imagined I was Felix and my mum was being sent away. When Mum walked in the door I hugged her tight. 'Everything okay?' she asked. Now she thinks *I'm* in some sort of trouble. Actually, I'm not very happy. I'm supposed to be working on my project but I don't care about it now. Athena dumped me for Matisse, who says she just *adores* Shetlands. It's a sad story and if it wasn't for Felix I'd be feeling a lot sorrier for myself.

What will happen to him? I keep thinking of those movies where the cops burst in, guns blazing, to find the bathroom window wide open, the curtain blowing in the breeze . . . Sorry, I know it's serious . . . but keep the bathroom window open.

Can I help? Like search for vital information on the net? I've put a spell on Maik, for you, long distance. He'd be the most unhelpful person in creation, right now!

I know, I'll make you laugh. Here's Danielle doing housework.

Danhousework.jpg

About being legal and illegal in Australia. Australia's an island, not like Germany, butted up against neighbours. Asylum seekers called 'boat people' used to pay a fortune to people smugglers for a trip here on an overcrowded tub from Indonesia, but when the government got tough and put them in detention centres for ages, on islands up north, they stopped coming.

We take lots of migrants, but Mum says there are many illegals who simply overstay their visas and melt in (like Ümit). About refugees, she thinks we take about 13,000 a year, at the moment, most of them from Africa, Iraq and Afghanistan.

Oh boy, makes you feel lucky.

Hey Felix –
Q: Why did the man go *up* the hill to feed his sheep and *down* the hill to feed his cows?

Keep that window open.

H

Berlin, Donnerstag, 20.Oktober 23.18

Thanks for your mail, Henni (and for the pictures of your little devil sister — they made me laugh).

I can't see me fight like a knight. I feel like a pawn, too.

There won't be guns and stuff. Just "cold bureaucracy", as Bettina puts it, treating people like figures on a board. On their board. And yes, they make the rules.

Nothing new. Everybody is wondering where Felix might be AND we ran out of money.

Now Felix has to rely on what is stored in the kitchen — no fast food, that's for sure. But he has no idea how to cook himself a meal.

When I got to the flat this afternoon there was smoke on the staircase and it smelled like hell. Luckily no neighbor called the fire squad.

Felix had tried to cook rice and had burnt it completely. The cleaning of the pot took him half an hour. Meanwhile I cooked spaghetti. We had them with oil and garlic and parmesan cheese.

Felix sulked all afternoon. Then I gave him your riddle.

He smiled, almost the old Felix smile, and said: "Gee, you have to go as far as to Australia to get such a baby riddle?" I didn't have a clue — I am happy to know that cows are bigger than sheep. I have no idea why go up or down to feed them. Felix said: "Because they are hungry, stupid!"

Tomorrow I will bring him the recipes Knut wrote out for me two years ago, when he thought that it was about time for me to be part of the kitchen squad.

Felix's got to learn it. Or live on water and bread. Well, he is a prisoner in a way, right? I have no idea how this is going to end. When I am not there I just try not to think about it. I stay in my room, play computer games, walk about the internet.

At least I can tell you. That is a lot of help.

Change the subject. Omi, Knut's mother, is very good at that. When she doesn't want to talk about something, she starts talking about the weather. (It drives Bettina mad. They always fight.)

Mashed potatoes? I don't think you need a recipe for that. Just cook the potatoes till they are done, pour the water out, add milk. SMASH! SMASH! SMASH! Till they are soft, fluffy and creamy. Add butter and a tiny bit of nutmeg.

Done. Me too.

Okay, Henni Penni. Got to go to bed.

Felix will need breakfast. Tomorrow morning I have to pocket some bread and stuff and get it to him before school.

I hate to do all this secretly. I feel like I am cheating in an honest game. But Felix insists that I don't tell. If I want to help him I must keep quiet. He is absolutely sure all adults believe in the rule of law and will be opposed to illegal actions like hiding someone who is being sought for by the police. I don't know, but I can't try it out, can I?

You know what he wrote on that little note to his father? *Dad, don't worry, for me it's noon now. Tell Mom, I am safe. They won't get us out.*

"Noon?" I said.

"It's one of the oldest riddles," Felix said. "In the morning it walks on four legs, at noon on two legs, and in the evening on three legs? What is it?"

Care to solve it? I don't have a clue.

Leo

The government think Nali is a pot plant they can just plonk
here, or plonk there, but people put down deep roots. It's so
cruel! I guess Felix's dad is desperate too, but what can he do?
He's not a citizen either.

How long can you hide Felix?

It must be hard keeping the secret from your parents.
Don't they notice food is missing? You must be a good actor.

I wonder if the Schmidts were illegal immigrants, hiding in
Cauldron Bay. Maybe Konrad was in trouble in Germany. No.
They planned to come to Australia. Konrad sure planned to
build the house.

Remember the letters I found with the Schmidts' books?
I've written to that Horsham address. I wrote

> *Dear Receiver of This Letter,*
> *I am trying to get in touch with any descendants of*
> *Konrad, Bettina, Gretel, Christa or Leopold Schmidt, a*
> *German family who came to Australia before the First*
> *World War. Their friends, Mr Bernd and Mrs Hildegard*
> *Mauch, lived at this address back then. I have letters*
> *in German, from Mrs Mauch to the Schmidts.*
>
> *If you don' t know anything about the Schmidts,*
> *do you know someone who might know? Maybe*
> *someone interested in history? I would very very*
> *much like to find out about the Schmidts back then,*
> *and now. Please contact me.*

Wouldn't it be amazing if we did find The Living Link?

(Last time I sent a message into the blue I got a postcard from a boy in Berlin!)

The stuff under the Schmidts' house would be fascinating to a great grandson or great granddaughter, and when the house is sold it will just go. (Three boxes have already gone – under my bed!)

Felix. Riddle correct. Because they were hungry. Five points!

I know the legs one. Baby crawling in the morning (4 legs), adult walking at noon – and Felix – (2 legs), oldie with stick in the evening of life (3 legs). My friend old Mr Nic says he's still 2 legs. Just.

My cooking puzzle is getting all the food to be ready at the same time. Last night I did the beans and broccoli first. *Wrong!* By the time everything else was cooked they were *dead!*

The car! Dad'shome!

H

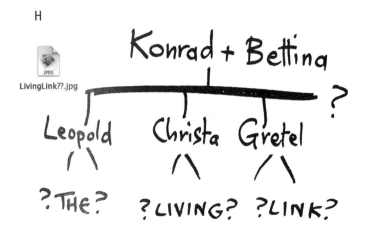

Berlin, Freitag, 21.Oktober 23.04

Hi, Henni. Nice to know that you are there.

Just got grounded because I came home late.

When I opened the door Bettina jumped at me: "Where have you been??? All I need now is worrying about you," she said. Boy, was she mad. "There are things more important then hanging around with your friends."

Bettina has joined the group that's trying to get Felix's mother out of jail. And to get Felix out of his hiding.

Yeah. She is right. I also want to get Felix out of his hiding, desperately. For a moment I was about to spill everything out. Then Felix's face came to my mind, when he said: "I can trust you, Leo, right?" So I just said "Sorry", went to my room and turned on the computer. To talk to you.

Great shock this afternoon.

Felix keeps going to the window, sideways, so nobody can see him. He was looking down to the street when all of a sudden he gives this little shriek sound and says: "Leo, the police!"

I turned off the DVD player and ran to the window.

A silver-green police car had stopped right in front of the apartment house, on the bike lane. Two men got out, put their caps on and walked to the entrance, with that official look on their

103

faces. Well, I didn't exactly see it from the third floor, but I felt it.

Felix grabbed my hand. I held my breath. We didn't dare to move.

"What do we do?" Felix whispered.

I joked: "Hey, I'll tell them I am Felix!"

He managed a grin.

Then we heard the footsteps on the staircase. Clonk, clonk, clonk. Deep voices. Clonk, clonk, clonk.

Felix shrank. He looked around and then he tiptoed to the closet and crawled in, behind Sascha's clothes. He drew the door.

The steps came nearer. What happens if I don't open? I thought. Will they smash the door?

Then I heard the bell ring.

The neighbor's bell.

Phew. I tiptoed to the front door, put my ear on it. The neighbor opened. My heart was beating like crazy. They were about to ask: "Have you seen a black boy named Felix?" I knew they were.

But no. The neighbors had parked their car in front of somebody's entrance and they had to move it or the car would be towed away.

Boy, o boy!!!

Sweat was running from my armpits like, well, don't know, like sweat, I suppose. I got Felix out of the closet. You should have seen his face. He went to the bathroom. And stayed there quite a while.

I know what can happen when you are really

afraid. Do you? They never talk about it in
books. But it is messy.

The weekend is coming up. Can't stay all the time
with Felix. Tomorrow morning I will have to help
Knut with the shopping — we always buy a lot of
food that will last a while. I will see we have
enough for Felix too. Bettina thinks I am growing
(I wish!). In the afternoon I have to play
soccer, just so I won't arouse suspicion. Mustafa
excused me last Wednesday. I told him I had to
stay with Lotte. He didn't believe me, I could
see that. I sure hope I can center a good ball
to him tomorrow. He's my friend. I hate to lie
to him.

Only the *taz* covers the story — our daily
paper (a small independent one where I found
the cartoon with the parrot). They support the
campaign to get Felix's mother out and her
son back home. Bettina collects all the articles.
She is very involved. I try to not talk about
the topic because I am afraid I'll give away
Felix's hiding place. He made me swear that
I won't tell anybody. Swear! Fingers up!
No Bible though.

Okay, enough for now. Read you soon.

Leo

That was *scary* . . . cops coming up the stairs . . .

So Bettina thinks you're just hanginground with mates –
well, you are, except one is hiding and the other is in Australia!

Danielle's playing tennis again this arvo. Without Dad. He's
putting the ladder away. Bad mood. Might come in any minute.
Want to send this. His boss is away and Dad's doing the workof
two. Hard. But nothing compared to you and Felix. If you are
grounded, who will get food to F?

Go Bettina! Stir! Cook the protest up!

H

Things got worse.

Being grounded was not the problem. Bettina had mercy. BUT we got Maik on our backs.

Yesterday Felix sneaked out. He felt so lonely, so stuck, that he went for a walk. It was raining and he put on Sascha's raincoat (big!), took an umbrella and thought nobody would recognize him.

Wrong.

Maik saw him, followed him up to the flat. Felix had to let him in. Then Maik went through Sascha's stuff, even tried the camera he found on the desk. He turned the Avid on (the computer to edit films). Sascha told me not to even get near the thing! Turned on the music so loud that I heard it on the street when I came after the soccer match. (We lost.) Maik clowned and mucked around and I just wanted to throw him out. But then he offered to stay overnight and Felix was happy. Even Maik seems to be better than to stay alone.

I made him swear that they would leave Sascha's stuff alone and that they would clean up the kitchen. Maik called his parents, telling them he was staying with me. Which they happily accepted. I am supposed to be good company for Maik.

MIST! (German swearword, English: manure)

Then I left. I had to be home for dinner.

I only went back this afternoon.

Maik was gone. The place a mess.

107

AND the toilet was BLOCKED. BIG MESS. Felix uses a bucket. He didn't say much. He looked so unhappy that all my anger fell off.

Shit. Shit. Shit. Ups, hope he doesn't have to do that!

I don't know what to do.

Do you?

Leo, in the deepest shit.

MAIK!!!!!!!!!!!!!!!!!!!!!!!!!!!!!!!!!!!!!
AND A BLOCKED TOILET!!!
Holyjamarolly!

You can put those chemicals down the toilet, like acid stuff that burns the blocked stuff out. But expensive. We had a blocked toilet in a motel room once and the maintenance man used an oompah doompah. I don't know the proper word for it. Like a rubber bowl on the end of a stick. We just called it an oompah doompah. He pumped it with an oompah doompah.

H

Berlin, Sonntag, 23.Oktober 23.18

WHAT IS *THAT* ??????
Are you there, right now???

    L.

takeThePlunge.jpg

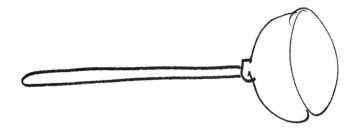

Look under the sink.
Might find one there. Or you can
buy one from a hardware shop.

Not expensive.

It worked.

Bäh!

I spare you the details.

Maik is a pain. But he did get food. He just
went into a supermarket and got it! He wears a
wide jacket and underneath a sort of hoody
with a zipper. He tucks ham and cheese and tuna
fish and bananas and chocolate into his hoody.
He even got a frosted meal! "It was so cold on
my chest," he laughed, when he proudly presented
his catch. He had bought three lollies, one for
each of us.

   Bettina keeps asking me what I am doing,
and looks knowingly. I think she thinks I have
a girlfriend. Taking advantage of Sascha's
apartment!

   Next weekend Sascha will be back.

   Have to think of another place.

   Difficult. Very difficult.

The campaign group: NOBODY IS ILLEGAL! is very
busy trying to get Felix's mother out. Maybe
things change soon. Though Knut says he doesn't
believe in wonders. He goes to see Mario, Felix's
father. Felix wrote another note, telling him
he is fine, no need to worry. He doesn't want to
call, in case the police is bugging their phone.
Mario is very worried, but he said to Knut:

"I just trust we taught him enough, so he knows what he is doing."

Talking about Felix, he told me to tell you this new riddle: A man wants to cross a river in his boat. He wants to take a goat, a wolf and a cabbage with him. The boat is very small, so he can only take one at a time. But the goat will eat the cabbage, or the wolf will eat the goat, as soon as he leaves two alone. How can he get them all safely across the river?

Got homework to do. School seems to be a very weird event. The History teacher changed the curriculum. Now we are discussing the matters of citizenship: who can be a German under which condition. First there is the "blood" principle — you are German when you are of German descent, no matter where you have been born. If not, you can apply for citizenship — under certain conditions. The most important: you have to give away the passport and the nationality you've been born with.

Just take it off like a T-shirt! When you go to your home country, you will be a foreigner. It's so stupid. In other countries people can have more than one nationality. There is a football player whose mother is Italian, his father German, he was born in Argentina, works in England in the Premiere League, and plays for the Argentinean national team. No idea how many passports he has, but I bet you more than one!

Talking about papers and nationalities, I forget French homework and do the translation for you. Here it is:

My beloved Bettina, my beloved son Leopold!

Since I don't know what is going to happen in these insecure times, I have hidden the papers in a safe place. In case we get separated, just remember Ting Tang Tellerlein. Then you'll surely find them. Heads up. We have come through much worse.

Embracing you, your faithful husband and father, Konrad.

No idea what *Ting Tang* is — "*Teller*" is plate, "*lein*" makes it a small plate — it doesn't make any sense to me.

Another riddle?

My eyes are falling shut. I don't even need to count sheep to fall asleep.

Isn't it funny that you are facing the day, and I the night?

Which is very true in a way.

Leo

Thank you, Leo, for the translation. I didn't think you would have time. I hadn't forgotten about Leopold Schmidt, and, to tell you the truth, it was such a sad note it made me cry. Konrad was trying to comfort Bettina and Leopold and sounded so loving – but I think I cried for Felix too.

In his note Konrad was frightened about what might happen to the family in 'these insecure times' so he hid 'the papers'. The insecure times was the war, I guess. What papers? What was going to happen? All I do is ask questions.

Where will you hide Felix when Sascha gets back?

There's an empty shed next door. Only problem – it's in Australia. There must be a shed near you, cellar? attic? empty building? above a shop? storeroom, underneath a hall?

Wish I could help you clean up Sascha's flat. Not that I want to impress you with my cleaning skills, it's just that it sounds like a rubbish tip.

Ask your girlfriend to help!

So Mad Maik is useful after all!

Just as well they didn't catch him in the supermarket. That would have been the end!!

I can check my email and send from Dad's computer at this time each morning, if I'm quick. Dad left twenty minutes ago. Mist! 8.10!!

Good luck findin g a safe place.

H

115

Where's Felix?
What's cooking?

The project bizo drags on. Miss Dakin has put me with Aidan, who wants to do *rugby*! *RUGBY!!!* (Miss Dakin says, 'You're a self-starter, Henni. Aidan can learn a lot from you.') Aidan's a no-starter. He won't even talk! He sits like a half-empty bean bag, staring at me as if I'm speaking Martian. Rugby is like British Bulldog, the game we were playing when I chipped my eyetooth. It makes tennis players look like butterflies.

As for Shetland ponies, Zoe says Cherelle told Matisse to do Shetland ponies to get Athena away from me. Who cares! (Me, actually. I'm sorry Athena wants to be with them.)

Okay, Felix, the answer to the goat, wolf, cabbage riddle: first he takes over the goat, returns empty, then takes wolf over, brings goat back, takes cabbage over but vegetarian wolf eats cabbage. Then goat, boat and man get washed out to sea and land on a desert island with a raptor.

Here's one for you, Felix.
Q: What's red and hurts your teeth?

And one for you, Soccerman.
Q: Why was the boy late for breakfast?
A: He was dreaming of a soccer match and it went into overtime.

Good luck Soccerman

H

Are you hiding too?
Hope everything's okay.

Dad: work
Mum: reading about university courses
Danielle: on the roof getting balls out of the gutter
Dinner: shepherd's pie, carrots, broccoli (not overcooked!)
Project: Aidan V Henni   Score: 0 – 0
Riddle answer: A brick

What's going on, Soccerman?

H

Leo, what's happening? I haven't heard from you since last Monday!

My imagination is a wild barking dog. I keep yelling at it, *Shut up! Shut up! Shut UP!* But the dog thinks Felix has been caught and you are in deep trouble. Just tap 'OK' and the dog will be quiet.

    You *are* okay,
    aren't you?

    H

Berlin, Freitag, 28.Oktober 16.43

Sorry Henni, to keep you waiting.

Bettina had banned any emailing, after she had got a call from three teachers complaining about my bad performance in school.

And ...

Shit, Sascha has just called. He'll be home late this night. Or tomorrow morning.

Felix has to get out of there. Your tip was good. In our basement there is a little room right next to the furnace. It's awful and small but it must do. Good thing about it — Maik will lose track. He drives me nuts.

Be back later.

L

Oh boy, did I *laugh!! JA! with relief.* I was positive you were in
gaol, but it was Bettina banning emailing!

And only *three* teachers complained? Who gives a
Schmetterling about teachers! I don't give a Knackarsch about
my project. (Your words are satisfying, like swearing!)

How's Mad Maik? Still leading his lawless life? I bet you an
Aussie dollar you won't get rid of him.

Surely by now someone *must* be taking notice of Bettina's
NOBODY IS ILLEGAL action group or saying stuff in parliament
or graffiti or the newspapers or   *something* . . .?

You've been hiding Felix for *thirteen days*! You've given them
thirteen days to scream and shout and make people know!

How long can he stand it?

How long can *you* stand it?

(Well, the alternative for Felix is being put on a plane.)

You know, until 1949, if you lived in Australia you were a
British subject! Then they passed a law creating Australian
citizenship. Also, after 1901, when the states joined together,
the government made laws called The White Australia policy, so
only European people could migrate to Australia.

My news. Miss Dakin wants to see all our preparation for
the project on Monday. I tried to talk to her yesterday at
lunchtime but she was busy. I'm going to fail, simple as that,
and I don't care. Dad's going to *love* my mark: 0/50!

Tell Felix to enjoy his new apartment! Yeah, I know – it's very
serious. I'm just glad to hear from you.

H

120

Mensch, Henni.

This is getting too much.

I got Felix safely to the little room in our basement. But spent the worst night of my life. And it's not over yet.

I will tell you. Be patient. Got some time before I have to leave the house to play soccer. I am so tired, I think I won't be able to kick the ball. But I have to show up there. I still have not told Mustafa. I don't want to get him involved. First of all: he turned fourteen, the age of criminal responsibility. Second: because of his cousin Ümit. I know now for sure that he doesn't have a working permit.

Well, before we left Sascha's flat, we started to clean up the worst. Too bad that you couldn't join! Thanks for the offer! But then it got dark and we left. Didn't want to meet Sascha and Tania! I went ahead, then I waved Felix to follow. He wore that raincoat again and was about to put his sunglasses on! On a miserable October day! I said: "Do you want to get everybody's attention?"

Anyway, we got to our house, sneaked down to the basement, to the last room to the right. The heavy iron door creaked like a hoarse monster. Spider nets all over. Nothing in the room but some dirty old cleaning stuff from the past century. Concrete floor. Plaster peeling off the walls. A moist smell. Felix pulled back immediately.

"No way I am staying here!" His voice was choked. He sounded like he was going to cry any minute.

So then I promised to stay with him the first night.

"Maybe Monday they let your mother out. That's only three nights!"

Yes, he is hiding for almost two weeks now. How much longer can we keep this up? No idea.

I had to go home and invent a story of a boys' night at Antek's place. I said I needed my sleeping bag and the mat. My parents didn't ask much. They seemed happy I did something "normal". Actually, they seemed to be almost happy to get me out of the house. Hmm. (Do you know what I am hinting at?)

I packed the stuff, put in a torch, grabbed something to eat — which I had to do secretly because Antek's mother always prepares sausages and potato salad when Antek has friends staying with him. That was quite tricky with Lotte dancing around my feet, all excited because brother Leo stays out overnight. I managed to take a glass of cherries and some cottage cheese. Fat dinner.

I walked all the way up to the corner because Lotte wanted to wave me goodbye, then I walked around the block, back into the house, down to the cellar, whistled the way we had agreed to,

so Felix would know it was me coming. He had the
door shut but not quite, and sat behind it on the
tin bucket he had turned over. It was dark, but a
little bit of light came in from the lamp in the
courtyard. There is a sort of window, an opening
right at the ceiling with a metal sheet over it
that had little holes. The light made little dots
on Felix's face.

On Felix's unhappy face. He saw at once that
I had only one sleeping bag. I pointed out that
I had two mats, so nobody had to lie on the
floor.

"And the cushions?" he said.

Cushions!

"Forgot the silk pyjamas too," I managed to
joke.

Felix got out the tavla board he took from
Sascha's place. We threw the dice onto one of
the mats, so they didn't make a noise. That took
away half of the fun, because playing tavla means
throwing the dice on the board and banging the
pieces from one point to the next.

Then we got hungry.

No spoons.

So we felt very Indian, using only the fingers
of the right hand. It wasn't easy at all. We made
a pretty mess. My shirt was sticky.

Two hours later — Felix kept winning the tavla
— we were hungry again. And thirsty. Very thirsty.

"Let's sleep," Felix suggested.

We put out the mats, lay down, covered with

123

the sleeping bag. Thanks to the furnace in the next room it wasn't cold. Felix moved closer, put his head on my shoulder, shut his eyes — well, I didn't see it, but I suppose he did. Because shortly afterwards I heard the steady breathing that I know from Lotte — sound asleep. And Felix's head got kind of heavy. I didn't dare to move.

I was ever so thirsty.

With one hand I could reach the glass and drank the last little bit of the cherry juice, but that made it worse.

So I gently pulled away from Felix and lowered his head onto the mat, silently got up and walked around the basement. Maybe there was a water tap. I dared to put on the torch light. And there it was: a wonderful lovely water tap.

But I couldn't get it open.

I needed a tool!

All of a sudden, Felix yelled: "Leo? LEO!"

My heart leapt up to my eyebrows, if that's possible. It was so loud that I thought my parents would fall out of their bed.

"PSST!" I whispered: "I'm here. You got to help me. Follow the light."

There he was, eyes wide open. Boy, did he look scared.

"I heard steps. I thought they are going to get me."

"Can you open that, brain?" I said, and showed him the water tap.

Felix shone the torch around, stretched up
to a little shelf and found the tool for the
water tap!!!

So we got the cherry jar and drank water.

A lot of water.

Next thing we had to pee.

Well, Felix was used to a bucket, remember?
But this was a tin bucket! And it made a noise as
if a church bell was ringing.

"Stop it!" I told Felix. But he couldn't.

Then it was my turn. It was not as loud because
there was already something in the bucket.

"And when it's full, what do we do? And if we
have to shit, what then?"

"Just don't!!!"

"What — plug myself up?"

We had a little argument, then we got our
senses back and thought we might be able to empty
the bucket in the courtyard, very late or early —
like three or four in the morning. There is a
tree and a flowerbed.

We tried to sleep. Slept a little, woke up again.

Then I saw the rat! I froze.

It was nibbling at the empty cottage cheese
box. A huge animal! I stared at it, stiff like a
stick, figuring if I moved it might jump at me.
I've seen that in a movie. I gave Felix a tiny
little nudge. The sleeping bag rustled — and
that was enough to set the rat off! It jumped

125

and hurried out through a tiny hole in the wall. We stuffed everything we could get hold of into it, and put a brick in front.

Then we heard the steps in the courtyard, right next to our window. But it was only Frau Klein, who put her garbage in the bin.

I had to stay till around eleven this morning. That was the time I had told my parents I would be back.

I didn't dare to sneak out to get something to eat. Too dangerous. On Saturday mornings the whole house is moving from here to there and from there to here. Shopping, visiting, cleaning, bringing the garbage down, kids playing in the courtyard.

Before I go to the soccer match I have to bring Felix a sandwich. He must be starving. I don't want to find a skeleton down there.

Henni, I — Verdammte Scheiße! Knut just opened my door. "You got a phone call, Leo. Sascha wants to see you. What did you do? Kill his hibiscus?"

O, boy.

Cross your fingers!

L

Sascha told me off, I tell you: How do you dare?
So disappointed ... I thought I could trust
you ... So you had parties with your buddies at
our place? How convenient ... I wouldn't have
minded if you had cleaned up! AND LEFT MY STUFF
ALONE! And where is my tavla board?

On and on.

I stood there, head down, sorry. At least the
plants had survived. Felix had done a great job.
And all the mail was there in one nice stack.

But that wasn't the worst.

When I got back to Felix, he was miserable,
starving, fed up, not willing to stay alone. He
almost lost it when I told him I couldn't stay
another night with him.

Then we thought we heard somebody coming down
the basement!

We shut the door, lifted it a bit so it
wouldn't creak, then leaned with our backs
against it. We heard a sharp metal click.

Silence outside.

"No one there! Stupid!" Felix hissed.

I turned around, frantically grabbed for the
handle of the door, and hit the bucket with my
right foot.

Great kick!

It spilt all over the mat, the tavla board and
Felix's hoody.

"Idiot!" he yelled.

"Schnauze!" I hissed. "They'll hear us."

But Felix yanked the door like crazy.

It didn't move.

We looked at each other in despair.

What now?

We can't cry for help, can we?

I tried to clean up the mess I made.

Then there was a scratching noise at the door. We stopped dead.

Then a cling, a clung, the door moved — and opened.

M A I K !!!

"Hey," he said. "Here you are! Shall I call the police?" And he got his mobile out.

I tried to grab it but he just put it into his pocket and laughed.

So, now Maik is there with Felix. He had followed me when I had left Sascha's house.

No idea what's going to happen. Maik is a wild-card. You never know what he is up to. This is just terrible. TERRIBLE. I'd love to wake up and realize this is just a HORROR MOVIE!

Henni, I know you are out there at the other end, but somehow I get the feeling it's just the keyboard I am dealing with, and the screen is but the mirror of my thoughts.

I am all by myself. Parents are out partying.

Leo

Melbourne, Sunday 30 October 8.33am

I just opened Dad's computer and your email popped up.
Are you there?

Berlin, Sonnabend, 29.Oktober 23.33

Yes.

Melbourne, Sunday 30 October 8.35am

Give me a second to read your email and answer.

Berlin, Sonnabend, 29.Oktober 23.36

Two seconds if necessary! L

At Cauldron Bay the surfies ride the waves, defying them, then – and this is the important part – in a split second they choose to fall. They let themselves crash into the turbulence.

You've got to tell someone, Leo.

Bettina? The cops might be suspicious of her because she's part of the protest group, but she knows what Maik is like. And there are two problems aren't there – Felix *and* Maik!

Or tell Sascha? Then he would understand about the flat too. And he might know a better place to hide Felix.

Honestly, if Maik hangs round, Felix will be found out for *sure*!

Tell someone. Don't you think?

H

Berlin, Sonntag, 30.Oktober 0.16

??? Call Sascha ???
    Should I ask Felix first?
    And Maik?
    Maybe you are right.
    Okay, I'll call Sascha.
    I have sweaty fingers. **GO, LEO!!!**

!!! I did it.
    I've kicked the ball, it's running now ...
goal or post or out?
    Sascha will be over in five minutes. Then
he'll be in charge.
    I am very relieved, no matter what I am going
to get.
    Thanks. Enjoy your Sunday.
    Leo

Melbourne, Monday 31 October 7.46am

Has the shit hit the fan?

It sure has! Ja, die Scheiße war am Dampfen!

Things did get kind of stormy here, plus my email server didn't work for a day, plus school stuff I had to catch up with, plus a lot of talks — that's the reason I kept you waiting.

Well, it's over with, but not really. Only I am kind of removed from the field and am watching from the outside.

Sascha got to our place, like two seconds after I had closed down my computer. "Where is he?" was all he said. We went downstairs to the basement. I gave my whistle.

The little room smelled like a toilet. The bucket was full to the rim. A lot of empty cardboard boxes, smeared with ketchup. Felix on the floor, wrapped in the sleeping bag, his hair stood in all directions.

No Maik.

When Felix saw Sascha, he jumped. But I also saw how relieved he was.

Sascha said something like: "My God! Poor boy, you have to get out of here!" And he directed us like a film crew: "Leo, you take the bucket and the garbage. Felix, you collect your stuff. Ah, there is my tavla board!" And he rolled up the mats.

Felix told me that Maik had decided not to stay overnight. But he had brought food before he left.

Within two minutes we were out of there, up in

136

our flat. That's when Bettina and Knut got home. You should have seen their faces!

Felix was sent to the bathroom, to have a shower, while Knut heated up the leftovers from dinner.

Then they turned to me.

First they kind of scolded me: Why didn't you trust us? You could have told us and we would have helped you.

Bettina was very, very disappointed.

I tried to explain that Felix was afraid they would get prosecuted, that Felix was afraid the police would search his friends' places.

"They did," Bettina told me then. "The police were here and questioned me about Felix and his relationship to my son, and if I could imagine where Felix could be."

That was while I was in school. She hadn't told me because she didn't want to worry me.

"See," I said. "You had secrets too!"

"True," she said.

"It's silly," Sascha said, "to try to protect someone by not telling them. That is like you are taking command over someone else's head."

"True," said Bettina to me. "I thought the whole time you didn't care what was happening with your friend, because you had a girlfriend."

"So you were all pulling at the same string," said Sascha.

Then Bettina explained me what the action group had been doing, and that there were lawyers

137

on the case. And yes, Felix must stay hidden as long as possible. It seems as if they won't deport his mother without him.

Knut hadn't said a word, but then he put his arm around my shoulder, pulled me close to him and said: "Son, in a way it was kind of stupid what you did, but it was great that you acted — it helped a lot."

Gee, that felt good.

Knut went to get Felix's father.

Then Felix showed up, all clean and fresh, kind of shy. Bettina had given him clothes from me, which were a bit tight and short, but better than his dirty ones.

He ate and ate and then we told our story.

About Maik. And everything.

Boy, it was so good to have it all out.

Felix's father Mario had tears in his eyes. I never realized that they both have the same eyes — a dark reddish brown.

Felix is going to stay with Sascha and Tania. Their friend won't be back for a while so Felix can even have his own room.

And you know what? They told me to update him (and me for that matter) on the school stuff — can you believe that?

All Sunday morning I thought about what Sascha said, that it is silly to try to protect someone by not telling them the truth. I went to Mustafa and told him about Felix.

He was cross, very cross.

No, actually he was hurt.

"I thought we were friends," he said.

I had to swallow hard.

Then we took a ball and went to the park. Boy, did I kick the ball!

I feel like waking up after a bad, bad dream.

But for Felix it's not over yet.

Henni? Still there?

What's been going on in your life? Is your world still the way it used to be? Upside down?

Leo

Ja! I'm still here dangling off the planet with my hair hanging into space!

I've been waiting . . . checking . . . waiting . . . checking . . . waiting . . . checking . . . then, finally . . .

Ping! Your email.

Phew, Soccerman, it's over! Well, that part at least. Felix must feel better. But he's still in hiding and still not with his family. Knut is right – it was fantastic what you did.

I've been thinking about Maik. Maybe he's not so crazy after all. He bought all that food with free dollars. (You are surrounded by people who steal from the rich to give to the poor!)

To Education Mode. My project saga continues.

Aidan was supposed to meet me at the Sports Museum.

He never showed up.

Tuesday was Melbourne Cup Day, a holiday, when the whole of Australia stops to watch a horse race and gamble. 'On horses they've never heard of!' said Dad. Then he had a rant about the evils of gambling.

Mum said, to put him back in his box, 'I fancy a bet.'

I read the list of horses. 'Hey, put money on Freedom Boy!'

So Mum did – ten bucks – and what do you know? Good old Freedom Boy came second! THANK YOU, FELIX!!!!!!!!!

We went to the quality pizza restaurant near the post office. The Upper Crust. Yum!

Now can you *please* find the meaning of *Ting Tang Tellerlein*?

The little rhyme in Konrad's note that I found in the Schmidts'
box of books – remember? The note that you translated?

Gotta run, my toast in my hand

GREAT to hear fomr you

H

Berlin, Freitag, 4.November 18.05

Hi Henni — before I say anything else I must
tell you that last Sunday our summertime was
over (summer is over long time ago — it's getting
colder, it's misty outside). That means we are an
hour back now. Adding your daylight saving time
makes it ten hours that we are apart — you as
always ahead.

School is out. Big soccer match tomorrow. We got
to win! I am in good form and so is Mustafa.
   Felix is okay, better than before, anyway.
The situation is still the same, but his father
visits him. They even went to the movies. Berlin
is a big city. And Kreuzberg, where we live,
is a very "multi-kulti" area. So you can be
green or white or black, Turkish or Italian or
Peruvian, Australian or Greenlander (have you
ever met one?), and nobody will really take
notice. We have Punks from Poland who earn money
wiping windscreens at the traffic lights, girls
in high heels and veils working at the desk
of the doctor, well-dressed business people
in fancy restaurants, and alkies (alcoholics)
with swollen red faces, sitting drinking on the
bench at the corner. Workers, artists, students,
inline-bladers, pensioners (almost no skinheads
though, the right-wing skins don't come to this
part of town). Here nobody will take special
notice of Felix, he just blends in. It's good

he can go out because he is really feeling like a prisoner.

A prisoner of stupid laws.

Bettina says: "If there must be laws they should serve the people, not the other way around." When we talked about Felix's situation in school, even Antek thought it was okay for him to hide from the police. When you talk about someone people actually know, they are much less riding on their principles — like "the law is the law".

And we still don't know what's going to happen to Felix's mother. Bettina says the place where she stays is full of desperate people who are going to be sent to a place they definitely don't want to be. Places where they might be persecuted, or put in jail, or tortured, or just live in misery. Why can't people choose where they want to live? After all, Australia and U.S.A. is full of people who chose to live in somebody else's land. And as far as I know the indigenous people didn't mind — at least not in the beginning, before the Europeans took control over everything. I've read a lot about the U.S.A. and the Indians, how they were treated and wiped out.

Okay, got a bit carried away. Now to your letter.

Yeah, I guess Maik is okay, in a way. But he only does things as long as it suits him. When he doesn't clown around, he scribbles in a little notebook. No idea what he is doing. Doesn't look like writing. Yesterday he did something completely illegal. He had been sent to do some photocopies in the office, and somehow he had managed to get hold of the questions for our next Math test! He copied them too, gave everyone a sheet so we all could prepare the test. I did it with Felix. The teacher's going to have a surprise — all kids coming up with correct solutions!

I forgot all about your project. Shetlands was out, right, because that girl dumped you? Now it's Rugby? Just seen it once on TV. It looked like a boys' fight got out of hand. Not the kind of sport I would like.

Ting Tang Tellerlein — I told you about Tellerlein: little plate. But I never heard the combination. I asked Bettina. Blank face. But she said it sounds like a fairytale. Maybe something with dwarfs? One of the seven dwarfs says: Who has eaten from my Tellerlein? Were there dwarfs in Cauldron Bay? Maybe the papers are hidden among little plates?

And what kind of papers have been hidden? Legal papers? Like the ones Felix's mother would need in order to stay here? What did Germans need then to be able to stay in Australia? Did they need a visa? Who could come to Australia in 1913? That was shortly before the First World War, wasn't it? What happened to the Germans during the war? Did Australia enter the war? Were they enemies? Gee, I know nothing about Australia.

But that little note I translated for you did sound kind of desperate.

I'll keep asking about Ting Tang Tellerlein. It seems to be some kind of a clue.

Well, got to go.

Leo

Hello Soccerman!

Yes, the project topic *was* RUGBY! Aidan hasn't done a thing. No project goal, no research, no organising of transport and accommodation, no list of questions, no nothing. He did ask one question – 'Henni, are you always like this?'

I'd chew my collar if I had a collar!

So, forget the project, I'm reading about Germans in Australia. Before the First World War we imported from Germany: wire for fences, railway tracks and pianos. (My friend Mr Nic has a Thürmer piano. (see dots!)

Lots of Germans, especially scientists, helped 'build our nation' (sounds like bricklaying!). The one I know was Baron von Mueller. He was director of the Melbourne Botanic Gardens, where there's a statue of his head, and his nose is shiny because everyone pats it.

Baron vonM.jpg

In 1900, Germans were the second largest migrant group in Australia. German migrants turned into Australians quite quickly. They stopped speaking German in about three generations. In every single book the German migrants are described as 'hard working'. Sometimes 'sought after as workers' or 'industrious and hard working' or 'honest, hardy, thrifty and hard working', but always 'hard working'. Are you hard working? I don't know how Australians would be described. Not like that. But we do work hard. Mum does, and Dad sure does right now.

I read that Australia was encouraging migrants from the United Kingdom but had the White Australia policy to keep out people from Asia. I guess the Germans looked the same as the British, same colour anyway. The government was so racist! I was shocked to read this quote from a German who visited Australia in 1905 – 'Australia can be proud to have maintained a continent made up of the world's best races.' !!!!! You can't say things like that anymore, but countries still act in a racist way. Refugees who make it to Australia get locked up like prisoners, like Felix's mum. Countries don't want refugees. Their borders are shut. Maybe soon you won't even be able to *be* a refugee!

Yes, Australia fought with Britain in the First World War. You were the enemy!!! Every town here has a war memorial with the names of soldiers who died. (I read that the German consul-general said, 'The psychosis against Germany . . . was stronger here in Australia than in any other enemy country.' I think that means hatred!) I'm worried about the Schmidts. 1914 was not a good time to be German in Australia.

Ting Tang Tellerlein is definitely from a kids' rhyme. It has that stick-in-your-brain-ness that drives you nuts. Little plates for *dwarfs* . . . ?

Okay, time to send this. Dad's off the computer and everyone's asleep.

Goodnight Soccerman

But I don't feel like sleep.

I'm sure the Schmidts planned to return to Cauldron Bay. According to Mrs Biddle from the store, they sold the house to Great Grandpop Barnett, so they had money, but they left their stuff under the house. So where did they plan to live? And somewhere 'the papers' . . . passports?

Goodnight Soccerman.

No, I think 'papers' means something legal. Konrad's note is so sincere. He thinks something might force the family to separate. You're right, it sounds desperate. I think something suddenly went wrong for them because of the war. It feels foreboding. I think Konrad is in trouble.

Bet I can't sleep
Read you

H

Things move. Bettina says the "Nali-and-Felix-
Stay-Here-Group" is getting bigger and stronger.
They have connected with other groups and have
stirred up the public. Now there are reports in
the papers, all in favor of Nali. After all, she
is living in Germany since 1979 and has always
earned her living! And Felix has been here all
his life. There's talk about a strike of the
school so Felix can come back. That is something
even I can do! Only Knut wrinkles his forehead
and says: "If they want them out, they want them
out. Bureaucracy is stronger than anything."
But he supports the group. He is taking care of
Lotte so Bettina has more time to do things.

Cross fingers. In German we push the thumb
between the fingers and say: "I'll press the
thumb!"

Felix says he feels as if he is living in a
soap bubble. He is watching TV like he wants to
replace real life. And he does all the homework
I take to him. Even with pleasure I think.

Two of our teachers are involved in the
liberation group. They check Felix's homework and
give him things to work on. I am the messenger
boy! I make sure that nobody follows me. The
good thing is I get all my Math homework done!
The teacher is very content with the progress
I am making.

Bettina is going to visit Felix's mother tomorrow. And she's going to take me! She called the jail to find out if I could go, and the guy said: "Yes, but it's not really pretty here. Are you sure you want to burden your son with that?" And she said: "You cannot protect children by keeping them away from reality!" Boy, she got real cross!

Okay, back to your mail. I didn't know any of this. It's funny how Germans are described. I told Bettina about it and she said: "You know the Turkish people who got here in the sixties were also described as hard working. I suppose people who go someplace to have a new start will be hard working. Otherwise they couldn't survive, could they?"

That's a point.

So Australians and Germans were enemies? Ha! Not anymore! Henni and Leo make peace!

Maybe the Schmidts were "illegal"? Like Felix and his mother? Maybe that was the problem?

Bettina says she'll look up a nursery rhyme book for Ting Tang Tellerlein.

Okay, tomorrow is the day I am going to see Felix's mother.

Read you!

Leo

Henni, I am back. It was terrible. Can't get it
out of my mind. I'll try to describe it again.
Because I have just talked to Felix, who squeezed
me out like a lemon. He wanted to know every
single detail. How his mother was today, what
she wore, did she like the book he sent her,
did she like the food we brought. You did take
Harzer Käse, didn't you? (*German sour milk cheese
made from low-fat curd cheese* — Wikipedia!!!
Fantastic!) Sure, we did.

The jail is at the end of town. We had to take
two trains and walk fifteen minutes along a road
by a river. On one side are modern apartment
blocks. On the other side is an industrial
area and a green belt of little vegetable
gardens. And the jail. A huge ugly seven-storey
building made from prefabricated slabs (typical
for the East). Attached to it a similar four-
storey building with rows of windows with bars.
Each window a cell. And all surrounded by a
four-meter wall topped with wound barbed wire.
It's controlled from watchtowers. A guard is
sitting behind glass — bulletproof, I bet you.
A fortress. I took pictures.
    You would think this is where they lock away
the worst criminals, but it's only people who are
not wanted in this country. Their "crime" is the
lack of proper papers. Their "crime" is they fled

from war, hunger, persecution, misery. Just the look of it made me sick.

When they let you in, you walk between the prison wall with the barbed wire and another high fence. It's like a tube they use for the lions and tigers in a circus. At the end you come to the administration building, where you show your ID, and tell them who you want to see. Then they go and get the person. Meanwhile they check what you brought. You can bring things that do not "endanger the safety and the order of the institution". We had food, juice, books and newspapers.

Bettina told me that Nali's friends have organized the visits so she gets to see someone every day, and she can tell what she needs.

We were led into a room with eight tables, green plants, a painting on one wall. It looked friendly — as long as you didn't look to the wall of bars on one side.

After five minutes keys rattled, locks opened and Nali was brought in. Big embrace. Tears in my eyes. Nali held me as if she was holding Felix. She wanted to know everything about Felix.

She looked bad, bad. Her eyes deep and dark. She smiled, listening to my stories (the toilet, the bucket, the rat ...), but there still was a sad wrinkle around her eyes.

Nali said she was lucky, because not long ago visitors had to stay behind glass so there was no way to touch. Nali held Bettina's hand almost all the time. And every so often she stroked over my head, my arm.

She said there are so many desperate people in there. She tries to help. She writes letters, explains bureaucratic stuff, files complaints and things like that. Sometimes people are let out — then they celebrate a party. But more often people get brought to the airport. Yesterday, she said, they wanted to fly out a man but couldn't because the passengers in the airplane realized that he had been forced onto the plane. They unfastened their seatbelts and got up. The pilot refused to start for security reasons and the police had to give up. If everybody did that, they could never deport people in airplanes. Unless they chartered one.

Nali also said that once, sitting in an airplane, a policeman had forced a man's head down to suffocate his protest. The policeman did such a good job that not only the protest died, but the refugee also.

Boy, I had no idea of all this. And it is happening right here where I live. Not in a far away country. Or in the past.

The goodbye was awful. Bettina assured Nali that they would do everything to get her out. So did I.

I never felt so miserable in my life. How can people make places like this? How can people work there?

Back home, Knut and Lotte had prepared a special dinner, because today is the anniversary of the day my parents met for the first time. We always celebrate it. Today it was kind of sad. We didn't even retell the story of their first meeting. And nothing new about Ting Tang. Knut says it sounds Chinese too. Big help. Lotte likes the words. She sings: *Ting Tang Tellerlein, wer guckt da in mein Fensterlein* (who is looking in my little window)!!!

Well. Thanks for listening.

Leo

PRISON 1.JPG   PRISON 2.JPG

Poor Nali. Locked in a cage. What a nightmare! But she's still helping other people.

Why doesn't Germany want her? She sounds exactly the sort of person a country would want.

It's good that Bettina cares so much about her.

Can she have music?

Strangely, Felix's life sounds almost normal, going to the movies with his dad.

I'm reading about the First World War. It's all nations, nations, nations behaving like kids in school – Germany is best friends with Austria-Hungary, so if France or England give Austria-Hungary any cheek Germany will bash them up. Nations cause wars. Nations won't let people in or out. Maybe the world would be better off without nations. Can you just be people in a place and not be a nation? You could be the nation of Not-A-Nation. I'd live there.

Mr Nic, from down the street, says if I knew what boat the Schmidts arrived on I could find out about them from the passenger list. Could you please ask Bettina which ships sailed to Australia from Bremerhaven around 1913?

Mr Nic also said that at the North Sea in Germany you have to pay to have a swim. In the sea! Is that true?

And remember the Amalie Dietrich book in the Schmidts' boxes? I found it on the net. She was a German naturalist who went to Queensland in 1863 – the first person to catch a taipan. One of our deadliest snakes!

Yep, Lotte is proof. *Ting Tang* is a nursery rhyme for sure.

Hey, I got a reply to the letter I sent to Horsham asking for information about Schmidt descendants!! A scruffy letter – been in someone's dirty overalls pocket for a week. The Schmidts' friends in Horsham sold their farm. This letter is from a neighbour, Mrs Flynn.

She says, '*I have a faint memory of a child, Gerit, I think was the name. I can't remember if it was a boy or a girl. There was some connection with Aboriginal artists in Central Australia. I am sorry I can't be more helpful. It's a long time ago.*'

Gerit Schmidt? Weird name. Could be the Living Link!
Is Gerit a girl's name or a boy's name? You don't have to answer. I know you're doing a million things.

Just tap 'OK'
Okay?

Henni Octon – legal – although I never thought about it before.

A riddle for Felix:

Q: What do you do with a wombat?
A: Play wom

157

Berlin, Freitag, 18.November 21.02

Question-Girl!

What a funny question: Why doesn't Germany want Felix's Mom? Who is this "Germany"? Me, my family, my friends? Everybody who lives here? The decision is made by the state and by laws a government had approved by a majority of parliament, right? Is the majority always right?

Knut loves the saying: *Eat shit. Millions of flies cannot be wrong.*

Tell you what — I have never thought about nations before. Only when it comes to championships in soccer. Then I am Brazilian.

I have been to a meeting of the group "Nali-And-Felix-Stay-Here". They were discussing emergency plans. For example: blocking the roads if the police want to take Nali to the airport. The group has a telephone chain, a kind of snowball system. When it's time for action there is a list of who is going to call/mail/send an SMS.

They also think about having an action day at school — do a project on immigration. Or shut the whole school down for a day. Anything to create headlines in newspapers, get more people involved. And they plan a big march.

Bettina is all enthusiastic. Knut still has no big hopes. "For the government it's a matter of principles," he says.

"For me too," says Bettina. "I want Felix

and his mother to stay in Berlin, that's my principle."

Mine too. But I agree with Knut. If you had seen the prison and all this, the power they have, you would think the same.

Still, it's good to do something. Even if it's only to make Felix and his family feel better — to make them know that there are people on their side.

I forgot to tell you, Bettina got a book about Amalie Dietrich — maybe the same book you found in those boxes? She discovered it in the Bergmannstraße, around the corner where she works. There are a lot of shops with things from people who have died, many books and photos and stuff. The Trödler — second-hand dealers — buy the whole household and display stuff like china, books, silverware and furniture in front of their shops, on the street. This book is from the year 1913 and is printed in the old German (or Gothic) letters — it's called Fraktur. Difficult to read.

Bettina didn't get around to ask the guy for the ships. Too much going on here!

North Sea! How can you think of a swim? It's cold outside! But your Mr Nic is right. In Cuxhaven they charged an entrance fee for the beach, in the part close to the town center, anyway. But the guard told us: "Hey, wait ten minutes. After four it's free!"

Brr. I am cold, I want to go to bed.

Good night, Henni. Or rather, good morning!
(in case you read the mail before school).
   Leo

P.S. Gerit. Never heard the name.
P.P.S. Almost forgot: your fun-riddle. Felix
couldn't laugh and I couldn't laugh because we
have no idea what a wombat is or how you play
wom???? Felix gives you this in turn: What's
the difference between a snake on the highway
(traffic jam) and a real snake?

   The snake on the highway has the ass at
the front.

   Sorry. But I swore to tell it to you.
What could I do?

Amalie_Buch.jpg

Must be quick – we're going to the market.

Leo, I woke up this morning from a horrible nightmare. I had to fill in forms in Fraktur and tick boxes to choose between Dad and Danielle but I didn't know *what for*! I still have a bit of the feeling of the dream.

Poor Felix must be thinking, Is it better to stay without my mother or go with my mother?

That's much worse than my dream.

I want to help Nali. What can I do?

H

MITTWOCH, 23.NOVEMBER

I only know, at the moment we can do nothing
but wait.

I couldn't do anything anyway, because I am
sick. I spent four days in bed, with fever up
to forty degrees, headaches, nose running, sore
throat, no voice. Bäh!

Bettina sticks to natural healing methods: no
pills — but inhalation of sage-steam. You stick
your head underneath a little towel-tent over a
bowl with brewed sage and breathe that stinking
stuff. Also lots of vitamins, hot soup, AND
Wadenwickel — leg compresses — ice-cold towels
around the calves, covered by a blanket. It's a
total shock. The coldness pierces your skin like
needles, but it helps. When Bettina took the
towels off, they were almost dry from the heat
of my body! The fever went down. I survived.
But I am kaputt as if I have played two matches
in a row. Of course no soccer training today.
No match last Saturday. They lost. Mustafa came
over to report and keep me company.

Bettina is in the kitchen cooking my
favorite get-better meal: cauliflower with yummy
breadcrumbs roasted in butter, rice (white rice,
though Bettina would rather have me eat unpeeled
rice) and two fried eggs.

I am going to eat in the kitchen, sitting at

the table. Just Bettina and me. That's rather
seldom.

DONNERSTAG, 24.NOVEMBER
Feeling much better, no fever, second day.
    Yesterday I didn't get back to the computer.
After lunch I slept and Bettina turned the
computer off. Later on there was Lotte and dinner
and soccer on TV.

Good news: NO SCHOOL!!!

Sad news: it is snowing.
(Very early this year!)

I LOVE SNOW! BUT I CAN'T GO OUTSIDE!!! GRRR!!!

Bettina said: No way! Then she grabbed our sled
and took Lotte to the kindergarten. They are
crossing a park and there are little hills for
the kiddies, and the Todesbahn for us! The death
run. Every fall the park administration collects
all the fallen (ha! now I know why autumn is
called fall!) brown leaves from the ground and
piles them along the fences and at the end of the
death run, so nobody will get hurt. They also put
a wire netting around the trees and lamp posts
and fill these with leaves, again to save the
kids. It is so much fun! Last year we went on

Xmas night. First we had a big meal with friends
and afterwards, past midnight, we all went out
and slid down the hill. We had only two sleds,
so most used plastic bags. It's so fast! But your
bum gets cold after a while.

Snow is so beautiful! When I woke up this
morning I heard some scratching and knew
immediately it had snowed. This sound is unique —
someone pushing away the snow with a "snow
pusher". I jumped out of bed and saw the thick
white fluffs trickling from the sky, dancing
downwards ever so slowly and quietly. Lotte
climbed on a chair. Bettina opened the window
and caught some snow for her on a black sheet.
The flakes melted immediately. Then Lotte caught
them on her hand and she licked them off before
they had a chance to melt. "Mmm, yummy, snow's my
favorite dessert!" she said.

The street is white, the black branches of
the trees are covered with a thick white coat.
All sounds get muffled by the snow. The cars go
slowly because their drivers don't want to skate!

Last winter we made a class trip to the Harz,
a mountain area west of Berlin, and we built an
igloo village. The snow was heavy, sticky, good
for construction, better than fine light powder
snow. We stuffed it into buckets and made bricks,
which we laid in rows, curving on top until we
had a roof. Wait a minute — do you have snow
where you live? Is there snow in Australia???

I will try to read the Amalie Dietrich book.

The pictures look interesting. Bettina explained me the letters. It shouldn't be too difficult.

You must be going to bed by now, I suppose. I wish you a beautiful dream of a frozen lake (without snow!) where you can see all the dead branches and leaves on the ground, crystal clear. Put your skates on and go, light as a feather, and fly with the wind!

Leo (wishing to skate next to you!)

You are a cheerful patient, Soccerman, despite Bettina's natural healing methods! Wadenwickel leg compresses sound like a medieval torture, and cauliflower – more torture! Cauliflower could *never* make anyone feel better, no matter how much it's disguised.

Mum thinks everything is helped by a good feed or a good sleep, but she also gives lovely back rubs and feet rubs. When we're sick we get ice-cream and purple jelly with tinned peaches. The peaches are in syrup and they're sweet and soft and slide down your throat like cool slippery orange fish. And from Patsy's Cakes Mum brings back a vanilla slice. It's a block of beautiful creamy custard with pastry on the top and bottom, and when you bite into it the custard squashes out, and the more you bite the more the custard squashes out. It's impossible to eat without getting it on you, and it can have icing on the top, or icing sugar, depending if Patsy's in an icing mood or a sprinkling mood.

Icing sugar reminds me of your snow. We have snow but only on the mountains. Mr Nic said it did snow in Baker's Hill years ago, but if you want to ski or snowboard it's about a four-hour drive. We haven't been because Dad is convinced he will look at the snow and break his leg. Three of his relatives have broken their legs skiing.

stuff.tiff

Vanilla Slice

This is a V believe it or not → **Vanilla Slice** oops!

A vanilla slice is like a geological cross section

pink lava (icing era)

Pastryozoic layer (late pre-icing era)

custardinus matter (volcanic)

Early Pastryozoic 3500 - 2500 BC (Before custard)

About that riddle — a wombat is an Australian animal like this

rear view

front

side

This is you doing the ancient Sagebrew ceremony

If wom was a game the bat would look like ← this

Leo

It's spring here.

Two days ago it was hot. T-shirts, shorts and thongs for the first time since last summer. 'Hello arms! Hello legs! Great to see you again!'

At primary school we had to wear hats outside in the summer. The rule was 'NO HAT – NO PLAY', but at high school we are mature and responsible (and sunbake on the oval!). Cherelle slathers herself with oil and tucks up her already brief uniform and stretches out and cooks! Athena is going round on the fringe of her group.

Draw the igloos! Come on, Leo, everyone can draw. Stick figures are funny.

The Todesbahn sounds so cool. Well, I suppose it *is* frozen! You know what I wish? I wish I could magic the friends in my street to your Todesbahn on Christmas Eve. Wouldn't that be great? Danielle would be down it in a flash. My friend Zev would be wondering how ice relates to electricity. I'd go spiegelglatt*splattt*! Everyone would be making friends. They'd just *love* it!

I'm feeling light-hearted thinking about the frozen lake. I'm skating effortlessly, floating like a bird, gliding over the ice.

I am skating next to you and we are holding hands.

H

HENNI!!!!!!

    FELIX'S MOTHER IS RELEASED!

    SHE GOT OUT THIS MORNING!

    Felix is back home. I'll go and see them right now. Just want to tell you.

    I don't know exactly why. I'll find out and write later.

    I am just happy that Nali is free and Felix can go back home.

    HAPPY AS COULD BE !!!!!

    We are having a party tomorrow!

    Boy, I could sing all day. With my cracking voice.

    I am off now, want to see Nali and Felix. Got to call Mustafa and Maik and everyone — bye, Question-Girl. Celebrate with us.

    Have a ... well, whatever you have over there when you celebrate.

    Yours with a broad smile on the face!

    L

Want to hear a funny story?

I jumped out of bed thinking, Wonder if that boy in Berlin has sent me anything? So I went to Dad's computer (scrambling over Danielle and the vacuum cleaner in the hall. Danielle likes to vacuum at times like Saturday morning so everyone knows she's suffering). I leaned over the chair and knocked the lamp against Dad's computer. *Dongg!* I straightened up the lamp and turned on the computer. *Chrrr!* Good machine! It takes a while to remember all its clever tricks, so I zipped into the kitchen, over Danielle and the vacuum cleaner again, to get some toast.

Back with the toast – over Danielle and the vacuum cleaner – and settle down in Dad's chair. But the screen is blank! Tap tap tap. Nothing! It's *crashed*! Press the Start button. Nothing! A bolt of anxiety goes through me. What if I've wrecked Dad's computer? Anxiety is upgraded to fear. I'll never be allowed to use it again. It's a new computer and it cost heaps of money. Try Start again. Nothing. I press a few keys I don't know anything about and immediately wish I hadn't. Nothing! What if I've lost the stuff Dad's stressing about? Fear is upgraded to terror. I'm feeling hot and breathing fast and my palms are sweaty.

Then nosy Danielle wants to know why I'm swearing and pleading and wants to look over my shoulder.

'Get *out!*' I yell at her.

'All right! All right!' she says with a smirk. 'Don't get your knickers in a knot. Just thought you might like some electricity,' and she pulls the vacuum cleaner plug out of the power point!

After I had killed Danielle again, *that's* when I found out about Felix's mum!

I went from   *Help! I'm going to die!!!!!!*
to   *Hallelujah! The world is beautiful*

I'm going to celebrate all right!

I'll get a super choc shake from the milk bar, and I'll sit outside in the sun and I'll lift my super choc shake in the air and I'll go, 'Here's to Leo for hiding Felix!'

H

Hi Henni — I saw you sitting in front of your dad's computer even though I have no idea what it looks like (or how you look!) and laughed!

Shit happens! If you didn't have Danielle you would have to invent her. She adds pepper to your life, doesn't she? Well, she did it with my life too, when she sent me that mail — *You are Henni's boyfriend* — cheeky bastard! I was about to stop writing. I am glad I didn't.

The party was great! We had it in a church, which had been turned into a community center. The people there support refugees and were very happy to give the room for our party.

There was lots of good food. Many happy people. Felix and I had to tell our hiding story all over again. They treated us like heroes, but I was just happy that it was over. And I think Felix is just glad to be back home, back to normal life with Mom and Dad. We both had some champagne! Did you ever have some? Tasted kind of bubbly and strong. Later I felt all giggly and kind of on the cloud. When we were about to get the second glass, Mario, Felix's father, said: "If you drink more, you won't get better but worse. Alcohol is tricky, because you tend to lose your sense of judgment!"

So I took orange juice. And danced with Felix! I must have already lost my sense of judgment!

There were also some speeches to remind us that

there are still people waiting to be deported.

There were people from the Flüchtlingsrat
Berlin (Berlin refugee council) and Grips Theater
("Brains Theater") who had made a play about
a girl whose parents had fled from the war in
Bosnia. She was born here. The police arrested
her in the school in order to deport her and
her family! The play is called: "Hiergeblieben!"
("You stay here!"). That's what parents yell
at their children when they don't want them
to go away. It's also the slogan of a group
that supports refugees, people in danger to be
deported. "You stay here!" — that sounds strong!
Bettina thinks of joining the group. I attach
their logo.

hiergeblieben.pdf

I tell you why Nali got out: Felix's father
Mario, who is/was Peruvian, finally got the
German citizenship he had applied for two years
ago, after his divorce. Yes, divorce! Even Felix

hadn't known that. That was (and is!!!) top, top secret! Eight years ago, Mario's residence permit was going to expire because he was going to finish his studies, which meant he would have had to go back to Peru. So he arranged a marriage with a good German friend to be able to stay here with Nali and Felix. After three years of marriage he got a permanent permit, which stays valid even after his divorce.

Now Mario is German (a very Inca-looking German!) and his son Felix too. And because of the big public interest in Nali's case, the authorities have decided to "tolerate" Nali for a certain time, so she can marry Mario. But her lawyer says: Since her son Felix "abracadabra!" has become German, Nali has the right to get a residence permit anyway.

Sounds complicated? Crazy! All that drama just to be able to live as a family where they feel at home. What did I do to have all this for free?

Today Felix was back in school again. He was kind of celebrated, but it wore off pretty soon. After the second break nobody seemed to care much. The History teacher was the only teacher who talked about what happened. She had Felix tell his story in class, then me. Even Maik joined in. He bragged: "Without me, Felix would have starved!" Of course Maik didn't mention the blocked toilet — he had done it, with rotten food! But that was okay, after all, he did help, you are right.

174

What's with your project? Are you going some place? Still interested in the Schmidts? Hope you are, because there is this little note here sitting on my desk and a book about historical ships. Bettina got it from our historian friend.

In 1913 a total of 505 people emigrated from Bremerhaven to Australia, most of them Germans.

The ships left once a month, on Wednesdays. By Saturday they were in Antwerpen, Sunday in Southhampton, next Sunday in Genua, Monday Napoli, Friday Port Said, Saturday Suez, Wednesday Aden, the next Tuesday Colombo, eleven days later Fremantle, Wednesday Adelaide, Friday Melbourne, and Monday Sydney.

I just had my fingers travel the route on a world map — what a trip! Forty-seven days, probably cooped up in small quarters. Storms and heavy seas. Vomit all over the place. Eeks.

The shipping company, Norddeutsche Lloyd, used many steamboats. In 1913 it was the *Roon*, *Zieten*, *Gneisenau*, *Kleist*, *Seydlitz*, *Goeben*, *Scharnhorst* — the "general-class" — plus the *Friedrich der Große* and *Königin Luise* — named after Prussian royals. "The ship's names reflect the militaristic and royal character of the German Reich" — says the note of our historian.

Okay Henni, let me know if you are still interested in the Schmidts' story and what else we might try to find out on this part of the globe!

Sailing away ...

Leo

THANKS FOR THE SHIPS' NAMES!

Am I still interested in the Schmidts?
Absolutely   *JA!!!!!!!!!!!!*
When I got to school this morning a kid from Year 9 came running up – 'Miss Dakin wants to see you.'

Anyway, to cut it short, Aidan has decided to be sick! Best thing he's done all year! Miss Dakin phoned him and tried to persuade him to at least do a report on a rugby match from his deathbed. (He didn't even know what he was suffering from!)

Miss Dakin said she was so sorry it had worked out like this for me. Could I possibly remember the first topic I had suggested?   *COULD I REMEMBER!!!!!!!!!!!!!!*

In a flash I said, 'The life of Leopold Schmidt, son of German immigrants, in a tiny country community, around the start of the First World War.'

Maybe you could give yourself a couple of excursions,' said Miss Dakin, 'to the State Library and the Immigration Museum.'

'No,' I said. 'I know exactly where I want to go and who I can stay with.'

Soon as Mum came home she rang Mrs Biddle in Cauldron Bay. Mrs Biddle, who runs the store, is interested in everything and *loves* to talk. We're good mates. Forms have been faxed and signed. I catch the bus from Spencer Street in the city on Friday 2nd December, departing 8.45am. I arrive at Bullandro at 3pm, where Mrs Biddle will be waiting for me at the bus stop. Mrs Biddle said it would be a real treat to have me stay. She hasn't spoken to her husband, Mick, but she says she can handle him.

I'm going back to Cauldron Bay. I can't believe it!

More news. A week ago I wrote to three Aboriginal art galleries in Alice Springs asking if they had heard of someone called Gerit. Remember? The Living Link to Leopold? I felt we might have a chance because of the unusual name.

Well, today I got a reply from the Pintapinta Art Gallery. They said they were 'not at liberty to disclose personal details, but have passed your letter on to someone who may or may not get in touch with you'. It's Gerit, I'm sure!! *Come on Gerit, write to Henni Octon!*

That ship information is exactly what I need! Straight after school tomorrow I'm going to the Public Record Office to look for the Schmidts in the ships' lists. Then we'll get some facts.

After dinner now.

The Biddles have a new computer, but I don't know if they'll let me use it. Wish they had a scanner. I'll email you as soon as I can. You can't get mobile reception there. They use the computer to send weather readings to the Bureau of Meteorology in Melbourne. They are weather addicts. They reckon Cauldron Bay gets more weather than any other place and that's why they like it.

I've been looking through the Schmidts' books and notes wondering what to take with me.

I have to interview three people.

I'm reading a lot about Australia back in 1914, trying to imagine what it would have been like for the Schmidts. I told Dad, 'If I lived back then, I wouldn't have lots of babies and cook and scrub, I would be a writer.' Dad said, 'Fat chance.'

One last thing to tell you.

Today Cherelle and her mob were talking about me (little glances in my direction) and Cherelle said in a confidential voice, just loud enough for me to hear, 'You've got to be *joking*! No boy would come within a million kilometres of her!'

And I thought of you and smiled. And Cherelle was so surprised she was speechless! Athena *laughed*, and she wasn't laughing *at* me, she was laughing *with* me.

At recess I asked Athena how the Shetland ponies were trotting along and she said they weren't trotting, just walking, because Matisse is as thick as a brick.

    H   smiling

NOt a Maid.jpg

Me in 1914

Dad says if I was alive back then I would probably be a maid!

no computer
no TV
No fridge
no washing-machine
no vaccum cleaner
No iron
no easy anything

Lewis Carrol
R L Stevenson
Dickens
Shakespeare

I will not be a maid!

Melbourne, Wednesday 30 November 9.37pm

I FOUND THE SCHMIDTS!

I'm singing, 'The name of the ship is the key
'cos everyone came by sea.'

They came on the ZIETEN in 1913. This photocopy from the
Public Record Office is not very clear, but it's THE SCHMIDTS
all right. And Leopold was 12!! Born in 1901.

I'm attaching my questionnaire. Any suggestions?

ship_Schmidts.tiff

ship_Schmidts2.tiff

PRojectQuestions.jpg

Port of
Embark-
ation
~ ~ ~ ~ ~
Bremen.
~ ~ ~ ~

Age of each Adult
12 years and
upwards
(no teenagers
back then.)

Profession, Occupation
or Calling of Passenger

Konrad~Builder
Bettina~nil~and shes
Mrs K Schmidt. Doesn't
even get her own 'initial.'

State
whether
English,
Scotch,
Irish or
Foreigners

19

NAMES AND DESCRIPTIONS OF PASSENGERS.

Port of Embarkation.	Ticket No.	Names of Passengers.	Age of each Adult of 12 Years and upwards.				Children between 1 & 12 years.		Infants.		Profession, Occupation or Calling of Passenger.	State whether English, Scotch, Irish, or Foreigner.	Port at which Passengers have Contracted to Land.
			Married		Single								
			M.	F.	M.	F.	M.	F.	M.	F.			
Antwerp	47214	Mr Jules Kennard	34.								Merchant Fireman	Scotch	Sydney
"		Mr F. Kennard	26								nil	French	"
Southampton	23461	W.B. Harrington			23							Irish	"
"		Bruno Block			12								"
Bremen	3003	Mr K Schmidt	96								Builder German	German	Melbourne
"		Mrs K Schmidt		31					9		nil	"	"
"		Mr K Schmidt			12						nil	"	"
"		Miss B Schmidt						9			nil	"	"
"		Miss S Schmidt						5			nil	"	"
"	25297	Mr J Brand	23								Boatman Engr.	"	"
"		Mrs J Brand		40							nil	"	"

QUESTIONNAIRE FOR YEAR 7 PROJECT 'GO AND FIND OUT`

STUDENT Henni Octon   **CLASS** 7 M

TOPIC The life of Leopold Schmidt, son of German immigrants, in a tiny country community, at the time of the First World War

APPROVED FACILITATOR Mrs Mavis Biddle, Cauldron Bay, Victoria 3919 Phone: 03 7219 6448

PERMISSION Mr and Mrs M Octon, 51 Stella Street, Baker's Hill, Vic 3771 Phone: 9744 5698
Mobile: 0409 2210 4572

What was Cauldron Bay like in 1914?

Who lived there and why?

How did people travel?

What part did religion play in the lives of people in Cauldron Bay?

What happened when you were sick?

What was the food of the time?

How did children go to school?

What did they do for entertainment?

Did the Schmidts have friends?

What was communication like?

How was Cauldron Bay affected by the First World War?

Did attitudes towards the Schmidts change when the war began?

What were the rules about Germans during the war?

Don't have too much time — tonight there is a
soccer game on TV — Champions League — the best
European teams compete and you get to see all the
good players.

So you are going back to Cauldron Bay — sounds
like adventure. But it's just history. You find
out how it was in the past, but will that change
anything? Take war for example — there have been
so many wars, and every time people said, no,
not again. Sorry, I've just watched the news on
TV. Shooting, explosions, blood. Lotte is smarter
than all these soldiers and bomb attackers. The
other day, another kid hit her. I asked: "Did
you hit back?" — "No," she said. "If I hit back,
he hits back, then I hit back and he hits back,
me, him, me, him — it never stops." I suppose you
could say she's learned from history — history
being experience? Hmm.

Well, hope you can use the computer and keep
me informed. Maybe you dig up a treasure! I would
love to go with you — and not only because it's
so miserable over here. The snow has melted, it's
seven degrees and gray, gray, gray. I think the
sun has decided to stay with you.

Here's your *Zieten*, Henni, from the book Bettina left for me. In 1914 it became Portuguese and in 1917 it was sunk by a German U-boat.

I have thought of some questions you might ask about the Schmidts:

- *What did Konrad build in Cauldron Bay?* (He was a carpenter, right?)
- *Did he sell furniture to the people of Cauldron Bay?* (Maybe there is a piece left you could see?)
- *Where did he get the timber? Off his land?*
- *Where was his workshop?*
- *Did he teach Leopold to be a carpenter?*
- *Did they have the Australian citizenship?*
- *Why did they leave?*

Knut is calling: They introduce the players — got to go!

    Have a nice trip! Leo
    Kick off!

the ZIETEN.jpg

Die Feldherren-Klasse

Bei der Barbarossa-Klasse wurde schon erwähnt, daß jene Schiffe für den Ostasiendienst zu groß und schnell ausgefallen waren, mithin meistens unwirtschaftlich fuhren, was übrigens einer der Gründe für den Rückzug der Hapag aus dem Reichspostdampferdienst gewesen war. Um dieses Problem abzustellen, brachte der Lloyd bis 1908 nicht weniger als elf Dampfer der sogenannten Feldherren-Klasse in Fahrt. Mit diesen Dampfern gestaltete sich der Ostasiendienst erheblich rentabler, und auch auf anderen Linien des Lloyd ließen sich diese Schiffe gut und wirtschaftlich einsetzen. Einige der »Feldherren« taten beim Lloyd bis in die 30er Jahre hinein erfolgreich Dienst. Eine vergrößerte Version dieses Typs stellten Prinz Eitel Friedrich und Prinz Ludwig dar.

Dampfer *Zieten*

F. Schichau, Danzig; Baunr. 692
8066 BRT / 9000 tdw / 143,15 m Länge ü.a. / 16,90 m Breite / 2 III.-Exp.-Maschinen, Schichau / 6500 PSi / 2 Schrauben / 13,5 – 14 Kn / Pass.: 66+44 I., 99+4 II., 130 III., 2040 ZwD / Bes.: 190

12.7.1902 Stapellauf / 15.1.1903 Ablieferung / 25.1.1903 Jungfernreise Bremerhaven – New York / 13.4.1903 erste Reise nach Ostasien / 25.11.1903 erste Reise nach Australien / Bis 1914 im Australien- bzw. Ostasien-Dienst, ausgenommen acht Nordatlantikreisen zwischen 1907 und 1912 / 1911 mit 8021 BRT vermessen / 5.8.1914 in Moçambique interniert / 23.2.1916 von der portugiesischen Regierung beschlagnahmt, umbenannt **Tungue** / 27.11.1917 von dem deutschen U-Boot **UB 17** versenkt.

Dampfer *Roon*

Joh. C. Tecklenborg AG, Geestemünde; Baunr. 180
8022 BRT / 8900 tdw / 143,79 m Länge ü.a. / 17,00 m Breite / 2 III.-Exp.-Maschinen, Tecklenborg / 6300 PSi / 2 Schrauben / 13,5 – 14 Kn / Pass.: 72+44 I., 105+6 II., 120 III., 2042 ZwD / Bes.: 170

1.11.1902 Stapellauf / 9.4.1903 Ablieferung / 15.4.1903 Jungfernreise Bremerhaven – Ostasien / 1904 mit 8133 BRT vermessen / 16.5.1906 auf Okinoshima gestrandet, nach sechswöchiger Reparatur in Nagasaki wieder in Fahrt / 19.2.1908 erste Reise nach Australien / 2.3.1909 erste Reise Bremerhaven – New York / 1911 mit 8174 BRT vermessen / Bis 1914 machte die **Roon** insgesamt neun Nordatlantikreisen, zehn nach Australien und 14 nach Ostasien / 8.1914 in Tjilatjap interniert / 5.8.1919 an The Shipping Controller, London, abgeliefert. Von der British India SN Co bereedert / 1921 als **Constantinoupolis** an die griechische Regierung / 5.1925 zum Abwracken nach Deutschland

Dampfer *Seydlitz*

F. Schichau, Danzig; Baunr. 693
7942 BRT / 9000 tdw / 143,15 m Länge ü.a. / 16,90 m Breite / 2 III.-Exp.-Maschinen, Schichau / 6500 PSi / 2 Schrauben / 13,5 – 14 Kn / Pass.: 66+44 I., 107+8 II., 138 III., 1940 ZwD / Bes.: 190

25.10.1902 Stapellauf / 4.6.1903 Ablieferung / 5.8.1903 Jungfernreise Bremerhaven – Ostasien / 22.2.1905 erste Reise nach Australien / 1905 mit 7964 BRT vermessen / 31.3.1906 erste Reise Bremerhaven – New York / 1911 mit 8008 BRT vermessen / 15.3.1913 eine Rundreise nach Südamerika / Bis 1914 insgesamt sechs Reisen nach Ostasien, 18 nach Australien und 8 auf dem Nordatlantik / 3.8.1914 aus Sydney ausgelaufen, Kurs auf Valparaiso genommen und dort als Hilfsschiff des Kreuzergeschwaders Graf Spee in Dienst / 28.12.1914 in San Antonio interniert / 1.9.1920 nach Deutschland zurück, auf Grund des Columbus-Abkommens nicht abgeliefert / Nach Umbau 192 Pass. und 474 III. Klasse / 12.11.1921 erste Nachkriegsreise Bremerhaven – Südamerika / 11.2.1922 Bremerhaven – New York-Dienst / 5.1928 Passagiereinrichtungen modernisiert, jetzt Kabinen-, Touristen- und III. Klasse / 21.7.1931 in Bremerhaven aufgelegt / 1933 beim Technischen Betrieb des NDL in Bremerhaven abgewrackt.

Das erste Schiff der Feldherren-Klasse war die *Zieten*.

Hello Soccerman!

This is your trusty correspondent reporting from Cauldron Bay! It was great to get your email here.

Thanks for the ZIETEN! WOW!! What a flat, skinny ship with one funnel.

The Biddles are so funny about their new computer. They aren't used to it yet and treat it like a shrine/alien/miracle/nuisance. Their eldest son, Dave (who works at the Bureau of Meteorology), installed it but he hasn't taught them much.

Outside the shop there's a sign with all the things you can hire, and now, underneath ROTARY HO, it says INTARNET. Mrs Biddle, that well-known light globe (perfect description, Soccerman, for a person with very sloping shoulders), hitches up her apron strap and looks at the computer – 'Yeah, we've entered the Space Age!' She's much more relaxed about the computer than Mick. Mick says I can only use it between 8pm and 9pm because at all other times it has to be available for weather information or customers. (I haven't seen another breathing soul here yet, except for the Biddles.) Mrs Biddle says, 'Use it any time you like.'

But it's not private. Their son, Craig, is hanging around. He's tall and quiet and a bit fat. He doesn't try to be friendly, just hangs around like a bad smell, as Mr Nic would say. He's the youngest Biddle, aged 25. Faye, their daughter, lives in the country with her 'little chicks', as Mrs Biddle calls her grandchildren, and Dave lives in the city. I reckon Craig is stuck – bored to snores and lonely. I'm the new entertainment. But who's complaining? I'm on the net!

Thanks for the questions. They're good.

186

Mrs Biddle picked me up from the bus in Bullandro and we talked all the way to Cauldron Bay. Mrs Biddle knows everything, because everyone goes to the store. She says there have been a couple of buyers come to look at the Schmidts' house and one of them was talking about renovations!!!!???? Can you believe it? My heart sank through the floor of the car into the earth's crust.

'Don't lose sleep yet,' said Mrs Biddle. 'They have plenty of time to change their mind. It's a long drive home, remember.'

We discussed who I should interview about the First World War times, and she knew about some of the characters from back then. She said there was a woman called Gilly Kneebone. She was a legend or the devil, depending on who you talk to.

Mick's not overjoyed to have me here, but I'm being the perfect guest.

I'm staying in Faye's room. Faye might live on a farm up north, but there's still a lot of Faye here. Her purple rag-rug is an island of comfort on the cold lino. There's a purple dressing-table with a cracked mirror; a narrow, rather saggy single bed (guess what colour?); and an old wooden wardrobe (no, plain wood!).

There are two things I really like. Mrs Biddle started painting the weather last Easter. At first she just painted clouds – Cauldron Bay has great clouds – but now she's getting bold. Opposite the bed is a painting of a storm coming. You can see a strip of blue sky under the threatening darkness. It's a thriller!

The other thing I like is the wardrobe. It's like opening a Faye time-capsule – a Faye display! Piles of fan magazines, a pair of rollerskates (where could she skate?), purple clothes shoved in . . . Her teenage stuff is jammed on the top shelf and on the door there's a mirror with stickers on it, and there are pin-ups of ABBA ABBA ABBA!!!!!!!!!

There is something strange.

I brought the pencil-sketch plan Konrad Schmidt left in the box of books. Can you remember? Well, the plan matches the Biddles' place – the hall and the rooms off it are the same. The shop out front is the large room marked 'Werkstatt' on the plan.

I've hidden the books and papers I brought with me behind Faye's rollerskates.

Feels strange to be staying here and not at the Schmidts' house. I went there, up the track to the stone steps and onto the verandah. I couldn't see inside, the blinds were drawn. Everything under the house has gone.

Tomorrow I begin the interviews. I'm feeling nervous about asking strangers my questions, especially as they relate to what happened a long time ago. But I want to know about Leopold.

Mick's my first interview. Mrs Biddle suggested it. She thought it might help him understand about the project.

How can you possibly say 'it's just history'? Right now it feels slightly explosive!

Question girl

Berlin, Freitag, 2.Dezember 19.57

Hi Question-Girl! Good to hear from you!

Okay, I agree, y o u r history does sound like adventure. Werkstatt is German for workshop.

What kind of connection was there? Did you ask? Did Konrad Schmidt design the house for the Biddles? I wonder what Mick will say. Did his grandparents live in Cauldron Bay when the Schmidts were there?

Today, after school, I talked with our History teacher about the Germans and Australia. She gave me an interesting internet link! I'll attach you an article on Germans in Australia during First World War. She said it's amazing how people tend to forget their own history. So many Germans have emigrated because of misery, or for political reasons, to seek a better life someplace else. But as soon as people from other countries want to come and live here in Germany for the same reasons, Germans say: The boat is full.

Let me know, how the interviews go, will you? I'll open up my computer every day — stay in touch!

Fingers crossed and good luck! Your man!

Precautions_Aliens_War.jpg

Henni !

Australian Government measures in regard to German nationals

Proceeding the war there was a rush by German immigrants to become naturalised Australians.

4 August – Outbreak of First World War

10 August – Government Proclamation

All German citizens must register their domiciles at the nearest police station and notify of any change of address.

WAR PRECAUTIONS ACT

This gave the Government special powers to make laws about anything affecting the war. Some of the laws affecting those of German origin:

(1) Publication of anything in German prohibited.

(2) Schools attached to Lutheran churches abandoned German or closed.

(3) Also German clubs and associations.

(4) Place names of German origin changed.

(5) A ban placed on anti-conscription statements that might hinder recruiting for the armed forces.

(6) Censorship of letters and publications.

1915

27 May – Aliens Restriction Order

Enemy aliens who had not been interned (locked up) ordered to report once a week to the police and could only move with official permission. Made to surrender all firearms, munitions, ammunition and explosives suitable for war. Naturalised subjects of German origin required permission of a senior police officer to possess a gun.

German citizens must obtain police authority for more than 3 gallons of petrol for motor vehicle or motorcycle. Also for yatch, carrier pigeons, telephone, camera or 'any apparatus or contrivance intended or capable of being used for a signalling apparatus'.

Justices of the Peace empowered to grant search warrants on being presented with 'reasonable grounds' for suspicion by police.

28 July – Amendment to Aliens Restriction Order

Germans and naturalised Germans must revert to the name they used before the war.

Any business must retain the pre-war name of that business.

Soccerman, what a relief to open up and find a page of your friendly type waiting for me— best typeface in the world!

There's a lot to tell. SO GOOD to talk to you.

Got your attachment about the First World War laws for Germans in Australia. I'm starting to understand!

I had another look at Konrad's plan. It *is* this place. I'm positive. All the windows and doors, exactly as he drew them. First I thought I wouldn't show the plan to Mick, then I changed my mind.

'Where'd you get that?' he snapped.

'From the boxes. It's this place, isn't it?'

'No idea. Never seen it before.' He had a good look at it. 'What else did you find?'

'Just books.'

I sure as hell wasn't going to tell him about Konrad's note!

The interview with Mick was pretty scary. At first he didn't want to talk – suspicious, sort of set against me – but as it went on he opened up. He knows a lot about wars, Germans, politicians. He doesn't like bosses. He thinks they're all rich. Mrs Biddle sat there listening. I think she was hearing some stories for the first time. She didn't grow up round here.

Then Craig slouched in and leaned against the doorway, which I found really annoying.

Mick was fine talking about Cauldron and his family, but if I asked anything about the Schmidts or the First World War he didn't like it. Mrs Biddle said, 'Mick, why do you have to be so hard on the girl? She's doing a project.' Finally he went into this angry rant – 'You don't *know* what it was like! Why don't you want to know what *we Australians went through* during that war, or the second one for that matter? *Who started* the whole shooting match? The Davises lost two boys. The Humphries lost a son. My great uncle lost his left arm and leg. That's why they built this store on my grandfather's land – give him something to do. And another uncle was so traumatised he never spoke.'

'Wasn't that the Second World War?' chipped in Mrs Biddle. Mick was lumping the wars together and she wanted to get it straight.

Then Mick really lost it.

'History's all very well, but I'll tell you what I think.' He stuck out his jaw as if he was picking a fight. 'I think you're a *silly girl* who's making herself *important* with this history caper, by *prying* into people's lives.'

'Oh Mick, that's a bit harsh!' said Mrs Biddle.

I felt terrible. I didn't know what to say. I mumbled 'Thanks', and pushed out the door past Craig, who was standing there with a blaming look on his face. Nobody's ever spoken to me like that before.

I went for a walk along the beach. Then I trudged up to the track at the top of the dunes, and right where I had to walk someone had written in the sand: PISS OFF!

Great

But I did learn a lot.

You asked would anyone know or care what their grandparents did? Mick knew heaps, particularly about cutting timber and shipping it out of Cauldron Bay. I was scribbling like mad.

One thing Mick said when I asked about Konrad's furniture-making, 'Apparently there was bad blood between him and Harry Davis, who ran the mill. Harry refused to sell him timber.'

'Who?'

'The German fella.'

'Is that why the Schmidts left?'

'Yeah.'

(And I just realised we were sitting at a table made by Konrad! Mrs Biddle showed me last Easter.)

Mrs Biddle smoothed it all down. She told me to ring Mum, which I did, but I felt uncomfortable because the others could hear. Then Mrs Biddle asked me to help her cook. She goes about it in a wholehearted way, chatting and mixing and telling funny stories about when she was a girl with her pet goat called Charlie, and how they made soap and candles.

The worst thing about staying here is going to the bathroom. First I have to go past Craig's door, which is always open. This morning he was cleaning a gun! It was in pieces on newspaper spread on the bed and a chair. It scared me. I casually mentioned it to Mrs Biddle, and she said in a very ordinary way, 'Yeah, they're going spotlighting tonight.'

'What's spotlighting?'

'Shooting rabbits from a ute, using a spotlight. They shine the bright light on 'em and the rabbits freeze. Would you like to go?'

'No, *thank* you.'

'No, not my cuppa tea either, but I don't mind a bit of bunny.'

The other bad thing – the bathroom door doesn't lock properly and the toilet is a long way from the door. I put a chair against it.

So that was Day 1.

I haven't found out about Leopold yet.
   But here's stuff from **PROJECT REPORT 1**. I'll make it neat later.

   Mick Biddle Born Cauldron Bay 1935? Etc
   My grandfather was the youngest of 5 boys. 'the Biddle Boys', lively lot.
   I suppose you've heard about Gilly. local midwife, nurse, crazy woman There were more people round the place then.
   The Crokes' house was right by Wishbone Creek. Got burnt down in the fires of '49. So hot all their jam jars all melted stuck together. Lumps of glass
   Old Mrs Croke taught the kids. A school was built round the 1920s near the church bythe bridge over Wishbone Creek.
   There was Catholics and there was Anglican.
   Like oil and water. Never mix. etc

What about the answer to that other riddle?
   ?????**T T Tellerlein?????**
   That's what I want to know.
   The clock on the mantelpiece is chiming
   dong dong dong X 9
   I feel like Cinderella, except at 9 o'clock and I'm not at the Ball.
   Read you, Soccerman

   Question girl

Hey, you really have stabbed into a wasps' nest, haven't you?

Maybe Konrad built the house for the Biddles and kept a copy of the plan. But why would *he* have needed to buy timber if the house was for the Biddles? They would have bought it. Well, I suppose he needed timber for his furniture. Keep looking for stuff he made!

I talked with Bettina about your interview with Mick. She said, "Same thing happens over here — people remember the horrible things t h e y suffered during and after the Second World War. And forget what was done to other people: that the German Army began the war, that Germans put Jews and other 'enemies' in concentration camps to exploit and kill them." Bettina remembers big arguments between her mother and her grandmother over that subject.

Bettina's grandmother (my great grandmother) always said she didn't know anything when they talked about the Nazi-time and the terrible things that happened. Her daughter Gina (Bettina's mother) always jumps when she hears "we didn't know anything". She didn't believe her mother. "What was it that people didn't know?" Gina says: "Are you trying to tell me they didn't know that the Jews had been kicked out of their jobs, that people had been urged not to buy at Jewish stores, that Jews were not allowed to

195

marry 'Aryan' people, that Jews were excluded from society long before they were deported and killed? All that was for everyone to see!"

I think Gina wants to say that all the terrible things had an "open" start. I remember well what I did — did n o t — when Maik was attacking Marika.

Bettina sometimes says Gina is too much involved in that Nazi stuff. I don't think so. Gina told me she was thirteen when she found out what had happened to the Jews. She said: "The adults never talked about it, never explained it. There was just silence. And when I found out what the truth was behind that silence, I was hurt. All these adults had been living at that time and I imagined they *must* have known something, or even *done* horrible things."

So silences probably happen when something has to be hidden.

What was it in Cauldron Bay?

Did they do something to the Germans?

They were their enemies after all.

Gina always says: "Every family has a corpse in the cellar." Ooh, that sounds gruesome. So whose corpse is hidden in Cauldron Bay?

Be careful, Henni!

I can't leave you like this.

Come and join me for a few moments here in Berlin.

In school we are preparing the annual end of the year party. The theater group will show

some sketches, the breakers and hip-hoppers
are planning a battle, Antek's band will play.
His parents will come, so he has to prepare them
for a surprise! No classical guitar!

I am part of the decorating team. There are
some graffiti sprayers who really are artists.
Maybe I can learn something.

There is one other 7th Grader in our group.
Guess who? Yes, Maik. I had no idea how good he
can draw. He even looks different when he has a
pen or a marker or a spray can in his hand. Open.
Happy. And he draws little comics. Real funny.
He showed me his notebook. The main character is
a little round thing with many little antennas
sticking out, and it gets always into big
trouble. There is one picture where the little
thing stands on a snowy hill, stumbles and rolls
downwards, more and more snow sticks to it, it
gets bigger and bigger and bigger and at the end
it falls like a bomb on a little village at the
bottom of the hill. CRASH!

Other than that, no major problems, just
the daily stuff — well, even that can sometimes
be annoying. Like the match this afternoon.
Rain drizzled all the time and it was cold and
the ground was slippery and a guy gave me a
Pferdekuss (a horse's kiss) — meaning he kicked
his knee into my thigh. That hurts! You hear all
angels singing! I tried to go on but couldn't.
That guy did it on purpose. The defence players
want the forwards to be afraid of them. They

can get so mean. Just to win. I hate that.
I like to win though. It feels overwhelming when
you've kicked a goal. It's like a glass of water
in the desert, like a good sneeze after your
nose had been itching, like taking the first
bite of a yummy pizza after having starved all
afternoon ...

Oh, Bettina just dropped in: You emailing?
    Yep.
    Tell Henni, I found the second line of
Konrad's rhyme. A client remembered it:
    Ting, tang, Tellerlein!
    Wer sitzt in diesem Turm? *Who is sitting in
this tower?*
    The next line was something with a girl, but
the client didn't remember it. Well — there is
no tower in Cauldron Bay. So that won't help.
But I keep looking.

Leo, from the other side of the earth. Wow, do
I feel far away. And close at the same time.

There *is* a tower! The platform high in the blue gum! That's *it*! More clues! Need more clues!

I'm walking everywhere, which gives me time to think about, for example, what you said about silences and secrets. Mick said everyone walked or rode a horse back then, so I'm finding out what it was like. (Did they think more?) But I don't know how long it takes to get to places. I was late for the Humphries.

Mrs Biddle thought the Humphries would be good because they are so old, and Bert Humphries has lived in the same house all his life. But it was like interviewing two friendly foggy old turtles. They didn't say *anything!* And everything in their house was cheap, from K-Mart about thirty years ago, and since then they stopped noticing dirt.

'Come in, dear. Yes. Yes. We're expecting you.'

My chair was set up facing them and the morning tea was waiting.

'Now, dear, how can we help you?'

Chat chitty chat chat . . .

'Of course my parents must have known the Schmidts,' said Mr Humphries, 'but, well, certainly if there was any trouble . . . they wouldn't talk about that sort of thing. Least said soonest mended.'

History is just a happy blur for the Humphries.

'Do you have any furniture made by Konrad Schmidt?'

'No, dear.'

They did tell me that the Biddles' store was built right after the war, with timber from Harry Davis's mill, and that Harry had six sons and the oldest three worked at the mill. Also the mutton-bird harvest was a big thing. Half a dozen families came to stay for a couple of months.

Now comes the interesting part – the cup of tea.

'Sugar, dear?'

I went to stir. But it was not your normal Cauldron Bay teaspoon! And certainly not your normal Humphries' teaspoon!!!! It was a heavy silver teaspoon with initials in script – you know, you have to sort of untangle the letters? Guess what they were? BS!

'What a beautiful teaspoon!' I said. 'Who was BS?'

'It's just a design, dear. A wedding present.'

Leo, are you thinking what I'm thinking?

When I was walking back along the track to the road, a trail bike roared past. The rider wasn't wearing a helmet and had skulls tattooed on both his arms. He slowed down and glanced back. I had my face in my T-shirt to stop from breathing the dust. It was Sascha's bikie, for *sure*!

After lunch Mrs Biddle was out so I was helping Mick in the shop. He said to me, 'I know where you're coming from. You've got this romantic fantasy about that boy, Leopold.'

'No!' I said.

Mick smiled, pleased with himself. 'Yeah, that's it! Leopold!' — as if my protesting proved it. I was glad Craig wasn't there. Craig's okay when he's with Mrs Biddle, but when he's with Mick he takes Mick's side . . . And when I'm on my own he likes to loom up, surly and threatening, and say things like, 'I saw a red-back spider on the wheelbarrow this morning.'

Later, I walked to the campground. I think I was looking for other people but it was deserted – overgrown, sticks and bark everywhere. At Easter the camp was alive with the surfies but being there on my own was creepy.

I sat on my favourite rock and watched the waves crash in and slide back. I thought, Am I making all this up? Is my imagination like the yeast in the bread we made last Easter? Making the flour puff up into dough that needs to be punched down again?

Mick sure is punching it down!

I tried to imagine I was Leopold, on the other side of the world from home . . . learning the language. And there's a war between my old country and my new country . . . and my mother's unhappy . . . and my father needs wood to work and is having a fight with the man who runs the timber mill . . .

I keep thinking about what your grandma Gina said about the Nazi-time – she was *our* age when she found out what her parents were part of. Boy, she's honest! And fierce. Does being honest make you fierce?

Please write to me
I feel alone, like Leopold must have felt.

H

I thought there'd be an email. Where are you, Leo?

I knew this next interview would be hard, but it was *horrible*. Mrs Biddle warned me that Maude was difficult, but she is important because she's the granddaughter of Harry Davis, the mill owner.

The track to Maude's was dark. The bush on both sides was a machinery graveyard, with car bodies and rusting engines overgrown by blackberries. Then I turned a corner and there was the house. It would have been impressive, for Cauldron Bay, but most of the paint had peeled off the weatherboards and the verandah sagged where a post was missing. Suddenly dogs set up a terrible barking. They sounded so savage I stopped, and nearly lost my nerve, but I told myself they must be on chains, and don't be a baby.

Then Maude opened the front door. '*Gid*-out of it! Gid-*down*!' she yelled at the dogs. '*G'on, git*-out of it!' She waved me to come up onto the verandah.

We sat down on two broken cane chairs. Maude was old – seventy? eighty? I couldn't tell – and reeked of cigarettes. She wrapped a brown cardigan around her bony shoulders and her grey suspicious eyes bored into me.

'So, what's all this about?'

I explained the project.

'Fire away,' she said, sitting back and crossing her arms.

It's extraordinary how Cauldron Bay people know the stories from long ago. They remember what their grandfather told them, or their auntie or father. Maybe they've all been talking about it, with the Schmidts' house for sale and my visit, or maybe nothing much happens, so when it does, they remember it.

'Y'see, Konrad Schmidt an' Harry were best mates,' said Maude, fishing round in her pocket for her cigarettes. 'Y'see, they both had an appreciation for working with wood. Konrad was a good judge of timber. Experimented with ways of seasoning wood. When the Schmidts decided to leave Cauldron, you know it was Harry that drove them to the train in Bullandro. The kids were best mates too, the Davis boys and the Schmidt kid.'

(I was thinking that's not what Mick said!)

When Maude talked about the war she grew *more* intense. 'The Davises were good Catholics. Harry was a strict religious man. They had six sons and two daughters.' She took a deep drag on the cigarette. 'Now Harry was a hard man.' Another deep drag. 'And apparently Harry forbade his two eldest sons to go to the war. He said, "I need ya both at the mill." He said, "There's more than one way to help the war effort. The country needs the timber too," but the boys were chafin' at the bit. They thought it was a big adventure. In the end they wore 'im down. Finally Harry says, "Off ya go." And that was it. Last time they saw 'em alive. Pozieres.'

I didn't know what Pozieres meant, but I didn't dare ask.

'I'll show ya the telegram they got sent, telling 'em about the death of the eldest, Ted.' She stood up and brushed off cigarette ash. 'That's all they got of 'im, a bloody telegram.'

She disappeared into the house.

While she was inside I peered round the corner, looking for the dogs. In the rubbish in the weeds I noticed something that looked like bits of an old wooden puzzle, all the parts separated and disintegrating. I saw an arched shape, a strap of leather, then a piece that looked like a nostril and a hollow eye. It was the remains of a rocking horse!

Maude came out and saw what I was looking at.

'Okay, nice to meet you,' she snapped. She slammed back inside and I heard her footsteps getting fainter down the passage.

What had I done to make her so mad? I plucked up courage and knocked loudly, calling through the door, 'I'm sorry if I offended you. What did I do wrong?' Then I waited, listening for the footsteps or some reply. But nothing.

Finally, feeling very uneasy, I stumbled down the steps and set off back to the store.

I was near the bend in the track when the two dogs came charging after me. They leapt around me, snarling and snapping. Oh those teeth! It was terrifying! Then I saw the tattooed guy standing on the verandah, but he didn't call the dogs off. Every time I tried to move they'd lunge at me. I froze in fear.

Then an older girl on a bike appeared. '*Go to blazes, you bloody mongrels!!*' she screamed at them. She dropped her bike, grabbed a stick and beat at the dogs.

'*Greg!*' she shrieked. 'Call them *off!!!*'

There was a whistle and the dogs hesitated, then turned, sorry to leave unfinished business.

'Mindless bloody *jerk!*' She chucked the stick into the bush. 'What are you doing here? Gee you're lucky I was round. Don't you know about dogs?'

'Not that sort.'

'Yeah, mongrels like their owner. What are you doing here?' she asked again.

'Talking to people,' I mumbled.

'What about?'

'A family who lived in Cauldron Bay before the First World War.' I felt weak and badly wanted to sit down.

'Yeah? Oh well, good luck.' She got on her bike and left me. As she turned the corner she yelled, 'We've got stacks of historic stuff at our place.'

When I got back to the store, Craig was leaning on the counter. He could see I was upset. As I went past him into the passage he said, 'Your project's a crock of shit.'

I said, 'Thanks, Craig, that's really helpful.'

Then I shut my bedroom door, curled up in my bed and cried quietly so they couldn't hear me. I cried because I could still see the teeth of the dogs and I cried because I was so far from home and I cried about what Mick had said, and because maybe I have invented one character too many.

Where are you, Leo?

OUR COMPUTER SYSTEM BROKE DOWN! I DIDN'T GET TO
YOUR MAILS TILL NOW.

When I got home last night — no internet!!
I was sure there was a letter from you, I knew
that you were hoping for an answer. But I had to
wait all morning till I got access to the school
computer. My History teacher let me into the
computer room after I had told her that this is
really urgent, and she didn't even ask why!

I have half an hour!

So I got your two mails — I must tell you,
it gave me goosebumps! I felt really sorry for
you — you sounded so terribly sad.

Do you think the guy sent the dogs after you
to get rid of you? But why? How can somebody like
you be a danger to someone?

Though come to think of it, country people
can be strange. Yesterday we went to a wedding
in this village north-west of Berlin. We stayed
all day in the local pub and ate, ate, ate. They
served heaps of meat (I couldn't eat breakfast
this morning, because I still had been full!),
and in between they played silly games. Like the
bride gets a parcel, she opens it, and finds a
paper saying she has to give it to the person
with the baldest head, and that one had to turn
the parcel to the person with, well, the most
beautiful legs — the most spots — the weirdest
voice (guess who?)! Embarrassing. But most people

206

(adult people!) laughed their heads off.

One guy topped everything. Three kids
(including Lotte) had begged money from the
adults and then sat down at a little table to
neatly stack their coins. They made a kind of
sculpture with the money stacks. Then that guy,
uncle of one of the kids, thumped his fist on
the table so all stacks crumbled! He just laughed
into the shocked faces of the children and walked
away to get another beer.

So, please watch out, Question-Girl. Don't
stack your money openly.

One thought, no, two:

BS = Bettina Schmidt. Is that what you
thought? Wedding present for her? How did that
woman get it? Where is the rest? If Bettina
Schmidt got silverware for her wedding, there
must be a whole outfit. (Yesterday the bride got
a set, and china, too.)

You know, Gina told me stories about how Jewish
people had to hand all their stuff to the German
state before they were deported, and these things
then were sold cheaply to the non-Jewish Germans.
Or sometimes just taken. So people actually
profited from the deportation of the Jews.

The teacher is at the door. Must close.
Knut said he'll get our system fixed, today or
tomorrow. So please keep writing. I will read
you and will get back to you! Which way ever.

Leo

I was so *glad* to hear from you! Sometimes this link is as fine as a spider's thread.

Mrs Biddle is my other supporter. She's always waiting to find out what happened. 'Well,' she says, hitching everything up in anticipation, 'how did we go?'

She likes to sit down with a cup of tea and hear every detail. She was furious about the dogs. 'That Greg! *Dreadful* man! Dead set against outsiders – hiding a murky past. How Maude stands that son of hers I do not know. And I don't like Craig hanging round with him. Only lifts a finger when he needs money for his motorbike. Those dogs nearly killed Ray Harper's dog when he went to tell them they had a tree down on their track. Ray won't be doing them favours anymore.'

Mrs Biddle grinned when I told her about the girl.

'So Sandy's home is she? Just finished Year 12. Hasn't shown up here yet. I think her parents are on holiday.'

Around midday I was in my room when Mrs Biddle called, 'Henni, there's someone here wants to talk to you.'

That girl, Sandy, had turned up again. She was picking milk and Cornflakes and things from the shelves and said in an offhand way, 'Do you want to see the historic stuff my family has?'

I said yes. Where's your house? I'll walk. She said don't be stupid it'll take you half an hour. We'll ride my bike. I said how will we fit? She said get on the seat.

So with me sitting on the seat holding the shopping, and her on the pedals, we wobbled off to her place. (Weird staring at the back of a total stranger who is doing all the work, knowing you are much taller and heavier!)

Sandy's place was an old mudbrick house surrounded by a bush garden hopping with birds. The door was open and a friendly mutt nearly wagged his tail off to welcome us.

'G'day Bozzy Boy. This is Henni, Boz.' *Wag wag wag* – this dog liked me!

Inside it was modern, odd and untidy, but nice. There was a row of old coloured bottles on the windowsill with the sun shining through them.

'I've got one like that,' I said, pointing.

'They're medicine bottles. My great grandmother was a nurse.'

'What was her name?'

'Gilly Kneebone.'

I nearly fell on the floor!

Sandy laughed. 'Mum says I'm like Gilly. Hate bullshit.'

I said, 'Some people say Gilly's a legend.'

'Yeah,' said Sandy. 'Not quite Ned Kelly, but big round here. Have you heard the story of Gilly sewing up the man's arm?'

'No.'

'I'll tell you sometime,' said Sandy. 'This was Gilly's house. Mum and Dad have added a lot. Gilly's daughter, Hillary, lived in the bunga. Hill died a week before I was born.'

'Bunga?'

'Bungalow out the back. That's where the historic stuff is.'

The bunga was a house-in-one-room with a tiny bathroom behind a curtain in the corner. Under the window was an old tin trunk, like the ones early settlers brought their possessions in. Sandy shoved a pile of clothes off the top of the trunk, pulled it into the middle of the floor and heaved up the lid.

'I've got things to do. Leave you to it.'

Leo, this trunk is a *treasure chest!* Whenever the Kneebones thought something was important they chucked it in the trunk: books, letters, recipes, documents, clothes, certificates, newspaper clippings, photographs, school reports, a tuning fork, a bag of buttons and badges etc etc etc – four generations-worth? five? I didn't know where to start. I decided to sort it into piles according to time, and Soccerman – I struck *gold!!!*

My first find is a large exercise book with a hard cover, all soft and worn round the edges, and on the front in faded gold capitals it says DAY BOOK. Inside, on the faint blue lines and pink columns, Gilly Kneebone has listed all her visits to the sick and the injured, the dying and the being born, and it goes for ages – from 1897 to 1938.

For example, in 1912:
16th December, Hannohans, Snake bite. Ernest died. 3 years

Sometimes there's an amount of money in the last column and sometimes there's not. In one place it says 'calf'. And at the back of the book there are notes, treatments, tables, measurements, potions, tonics etc. There are many many entries for Schmidt, Bettina. She was sick, all right! TB. What's TB?

The next treasure: in a bundle of Hillary's things I found a leather-covered autograph book with gold edging and soft pink, blue and cream pages. Lots of people have written autographs. I recognise many names.

And here's the best one – you won't believe this, Soccerman – in the same bundle there was a dark blue leather-bound notebook. Nothing on the outside, but inside the front cover this inscription is written very beautifully: To Leopold from Hillary.

(My hair prickled!!)

The first page was blank, but the next page was covered in handwriting – *in German!* (I went cold.)

It's Leopold's diary!   *This is Leopold!*

I tell you, my heart missed about sixteen beats!!!!

I can't read a word of it but I think you will be able to. It's in pencil, not the same pencil all the time. It's not a day-by-day diary. It goes over a few years. Then I thought, What if it's dull? You know – 'I got up and had breakfast. Today is windy. The hens laid two eggs.' What if he's boring and doesn't talk about their life? I decided, whatever he's saying, it's *him* – his thoughts, his voice. *Now* we'll see if Leopold's a fantasy.

I turned the page and there was a sketch of a possum eating an apple on the rail of the verandah. I *know* the table he was sitting at! I *know* that verandah rail! I know the great great great great great great great grandson of that possum!!!! I was so engrossed that when Sandy came back I jumped. I felt embarrassed.

'Boy, you're really getting into it!' she said.

'Yes.'

'Do me a favour?' she said, in her blunt way.

'Sure.'

'Look after Boz for two nights?'

'Sure.'

'There's a holiday job in Bull and I really want it.'

My head was spinning. 'Are you on the net?'

'Yep.'

'Can I use it?'

'Yep.'

'Got a scanner?'

'Yep.'

'Thank you *so* much.'

'One good turn deserves another.'

I sat down in front of their computer.

'Hold on,' she goes, spitting on her shirt tail and rubbing the screen. 'A couple of fly specks. I keep trying to delete them.'

Soccerman, I've scanned the first entry in Leopold's diary so you can translate it. Didn't know which page to pick, but people usually try hard at the start. I hope it's not difficult.

Sandy says I can use the computer and scanner anytime, and I've borrowed her mum's bike. Just have to feed Boz and take him for a walk. Sandy's leaving tomorrow morning.

Phew!!

Any progress on TTT?

Now all I need is a month to go through the trunk! Wish you could see it all.

Sending this now so you can get working.

I cannot *believe* how the tide has turned!

What does he say?

Yours
?girl

LeopoldsDIARY.jpg

Donnerstag, 14. Mai 1914

Erster Jahrestag in Cauldron Bay.

Hillary hat mir heute morgen dieses Tagebuch geschenkt. Leider gehen wir nicht mehr zusammen zur Schule, weil ich bei Vater eine Lehre angefangen habe. Ich werde Tischler wie er.

Aber wir laufen manchmal zusammen zum Strand Hillary und ich. Wir reden über unsere Träume und unsere Zukunft.

Vor ein paar Tagen kam eine große Kiste aus Deutschland. Großvater hat Gretel zu ihrem Geburtstag ein Schaukelpferd geschickt. Gretel schaukelt den ganzen Tag.

Mutter hat geweint.

Gestern habe ich ein neues Hühnerhaus gebaut, mit dem Holz von der Kiste. Christa will die Hühner füttern jeden Tag vor der Schule, hat sie versprochen.

Vater ist gut im Geschäft. Er will die Weide kaufen, auf der unsere beiden Kühe stehen, damit wir uns vergrößern können. Schließlich sind wir jetzt zu zweit in der Werkstatt.

Mehr fällt mir jetzt nicht ein. Hillary hat gesagt, ich soll alles Wichtige aufschreiben.

Was ist wichtig?

Berlin, Dienstag, 6.Dezember 17.31

We're back on the net!

Wow! What a found! Real documents, the kind historians use.

Listen, Henni — as long as you are in Cauldron Bay I will open my computer every morning around seven (I leave for school around twenty to eight). That's 5pm for you. If there is anything urgent you must know — I could go for it. I am out of school around 4pm, sometimes earlier (like today). So when you get this mail, it will be in the middle of the night for you — so let's say, you'll get it first thing in the morning.

When you then answer me — let's say around 8 or 9am — I will get it immediately, my time being 10 or 11pm. Got it?

Okay, will try to tell you in English what I read in German. Hope I can pick up the character of Leopold's writing. Feels strange to peek into somebody's diary.

(By the way, do you write a diary? I sometimes just mark a thought or something I want to remember in a beautiful calendar I got for Xmas from Gina. It's hidden in the back of my desk — it's an old desk Knut found on a tip and restored. It has a secret drawer!)

Here is Leopold, in his own voice:

Thursday, 14th May 1914

First year anniversary in Cauldron Bay.

  *This morning, Hillary gave me this diary
as a present. Unfortunately we don't meet
at school any longer, because I started an
apprenticeship with father. I am going to be
a carpenter like him.*

  *But sometimes we walk down to the beach
together, Hillary and me. We talk about our
dreams and our future.*

  *A few days ago a huge box arrived from
Berlin. Grandpa has sent a rocking horse
for Gretel's fifth birthday. Gretel is rocking
all day.*

  Mother cried.

  *Yesterday I built a new henhouse with the
wood from the box. Christa has promised
to feed the hens every day before she goes
to school.*

  *Father's business is going well. He wants to
buy the paddock where we have our two cows,
so we can enlarge. After all, there are now two
people working in the workshop!*

  *I can't think of anymore now. Hillary has
said I should write down everything of
importance.*

  What is of importance?

Good question there, Leopold!
  There's the rocking horse!

TTT? I have completely forgotten about that. I'll call my Omi right now.

No, she isn't home. I left a message on her machine.

Mustafa just walked in. We have an indoor soccer match today. He says: Hello Australia! He knows someone who knows someone who has relatives in Australia, in — yes, in Melbourne! People from his grandfather's village. Remember the Small-World-Hypothesis: six degrees of separation? They might live around your corner!

Tschüs Henni! Can't wait for the next news!

Leo

Hillary is Leopold's sweetheart! And at thirteen they were talking about life together!!!!

What a serious fellow.

Yes, Gretel's rocking horse for *sure*! Now I know why Maude got in a stink. The Schmidts' stuff must be scattered all through these hills!

By 'Grandpa' he means Bettina's father, don't you think? Otherwise why would she be so upset? And to send a rocking horse to Australia – that would be expensive. I think Grandpa is rich. I was disappointed when Leopold said he was going to be a carpenter. I wanted him to be something brainy. Somehow Leopold strikes me as sad, yet he's looking forward. They want to buy the paddock. Wonder where that was? They were doing pretty well considering they'd only been in Cauldron a year. Or maybe that was the first anniversary of Hillary and Leopold.

It was like a miracle getting your translation! I watched the paper come out of the printer then took it to the bunga – *Hillary's* bunga! I got goosebumps sitting in her room reading it!

The First World War started in August 1914, but Leopold doesn't say anything about trouble brewing. Maybe the war didn't affect them.

There are several pieces of Konrad's furniture here in Sandy's house – a small table, a big table, a little desk and, in the bathroom, a small beautiful medicine cupboard that cuts across the corner. Sandy says it's the last thing Konrad made in Cauldron.

Yes, I kept a diary, on my first school camp. Wrote down everything we ate. Hilary said write what's important. I guess food was important.

Our emails are like a diary—a northsouth hotcold nightday diary!

Boy, Gilly Kneebone was *tough*! She was a nurse in the Boer War. In one letter home she tells about ripping up her petticoats for bandages, and she rages at the way the officers and the medical staff treat the nurses as little more than ignorant servants. And she *hates* conscription! I found three letters she'd written to the newspaper about it, but they wouldn't publish them. Then she rages about Free Speech!

I haven't told the Biddles any of this. Time is precious now. I've already been in Cauldron Bay five days and I was only supposed to be here for three. I've lost track of time. Mum and Dad won't mind, they're so busy. Mick's trying to raise the pump from the well, and when he gets it up it's going to Bullandro for repair, and that's when I go home. Sandy and her parents will come back soon.

I'm spending every second in the bunga.

Boz is lying near the door. He has one expression – 'Walk?'

Here's another entry.

Go Leo! Translate with the speed of lightning!

LEOPOLDDiary2.jpg

19. Juni 1915

Wieder kein Holz von der Sägemühle
bekommen. Wir haben noch etwas gelagert,
aber lange reicht das nicht.
Harry Davis hat gesagt Vater muß
sich ab sofort einmal in der Woche bei
der Polizei in Bullandbra melden. Eine
neue Vorschrift für alle Deutschen. Ich
glaube nicht daß Vater sich dran hält. Denn
dann würde er pro Woche zwei Arbeitstage
verlieren.
Bernd Mauch ist immer... worden.
Vater sagt wenn sie ihn holen überlebt
Mutter das nicht. Und ich? Was mache ich
dann mit dem Mädchen?
Jedel ist gestern weinend aus der
Schule gekommen. Sie sagt die anderen
Kinder spielen nicht mehr mit ihr und
rufen ihr Schimpfworte hinterher. Christa
sagt nichts aber ich weiß daß sie die Zähne
zusammenbeißt. Mutter sagt wir können
froh sein daß Frs. Crofe die beiden noch
unterrichtet. Ich würde am liebsten anfangen
und alle verhauen. Aber dann wird alles
nur noch schlimmer.

Edward Hull ist gefallen, in Frankreich.
Der hat so gerne Vögel... gesammelt.
Vater hat ihm geholfen sie zu bestimmen.
Ich habe seine Mutter gesehen aber mich
nicht getraut sie anzusprechen. Ich weiß nicht
ob sie auch denkt daß wir ihre Feinde sind.
Morgen treffe ich Hillary da kann
ich sagen was ich will. In der Fabrikküche
am Strand sieht uns keiner. Und der
Krieg ist ganz weit weg. Sie hat gefragt
was für ein Pferd ich auf unserer Farm
haben will. Ich sage es jetzt: Eine graue
Stute mit einem weißen Fleck auf der Stirn.

Okay, Henni: With the speed of lightning — and
I must be fast, because today is soccer training.
And I'm all worn from the indoor soccer — that's
so much faster and much more intense!

Here is Leopold's German voice in Leo's
English voice:

19th June 1915

*Again no wood from the mill for us. We have
stored some, but that won't last long.*

*Harry Davis said father has to report at
the police station in Bullandro once a week.
A new order for all Germans. I don't think
father will stick to it. Because if he did, he
would lose two work days a week.*

*Bernd Mauch has been interned. Father
said if they come and get him, mother won't
survive it. And me? What am I going to do
with the girls?*

*Yesterday Gretel came home from Mrs.
Croke's crying. She says the other children
refuse to play with her and call her names.
Christa keeps quiet, but I know she's gritting
her teeth. Mother says we are lucky that Mrs.
Croke will still teach them. I feel like going
there and beat them all up. But that would
only make things worse.*

220

Edward Mull was killed in France. He loved to collect birds' eggs, and Father would help him identify them. I saw his mother, but did not dare to talk to her. I don't know if she also thinks we are her enemies.

Tomorrow I am going to meet Hillary in the little cave between the rocks at the beach. Nobody can see us there. And the war is far, far away. She asked me what kind of horse I would want on our farm. I know now: a gray mare with a white spot on the forehead.

It sounds as if the war did affect them. Wasn't Harry Davis the guy that owned the mill? His sons died in the war? Poor Leopold. Hope his father didn't get interned. I wouldn't know what to do if I had to take care of Lotte. And that's only o n e little girl.

And that little girl wants me to open up the milk bottle for her.

Good luck, Henni! Don't forget I am online with you!!!

Leo

P.S. How come you think Leopold is not brainy? Ever designed and built a piece of furniture?

Oh! It's *awful!* Maybe Konrad *was* interned.
Oh God, what are we going to find, Leo?
It must have been a terrible, unhappy time.
The Davis boys, Edward Mull – they went off to war and were
gone – just like that!
And in Cauldron Bay everyone knows everyone.
But they *didn' t know the Schmidts*!

I sit in a sea of paper wondering what sad thing I'll find next.
I checked Gilly's Day Book round the time of Leopold's last diary
entry, 11th January, and sure enough:

2nd January 1916, Schmidt, Leopold 14 years   burns

Here is Leopold's last entry, nine days after Gilly treated him.
Only some pressed flowers in the empty pages after that.
I feel sick in the stomach.
Something bad is coming.

?g

3rdLeoDiary.jpg

11. Januar 1916

Schreiben kann ich wieder. Aber arbeiten immer noch nicht.

Vater muß alleine zurecht kommen. Ich glaube er will weg hier.

Wo sollen wir hin?

Ich kann nicht aufschreiben, was geschehen ist. Ich werde es auf ewig in mir vergraben. Aber die Gesichter der Jungen, die werde ich für immer vor mir sehen. Und auch die von allen anderen, für die wir auf einmal Feinde sind. Sie behaupten Vater wäre ein Spion wegen seines Ausgucks! Dabei hat Vater Deutschland verlassen, weil er mit dem Deutschen Reich und dem Kaiser nichts mehr zu tun haben wollte!

Hillary hat mich besucht. Sie ist mir treu geblieben, obwohl alle gegen uns sind. Ihre Mutter hat mich gerettet. Jeden Tag hat sie meine Wunden versorgt. Ich glaube wenn sie nicht gewesen wäre, hätte Mutter das alles bestimmt nicht durchgehalten.

Vielleicht keiner von uns.

Sie bringt sogar die Mädchen zum Lachen.

Das Paradies ist nun endgültig zur Hölle geworden.

Good morning Henni! Bettina serves me my breakfast at the computer. And she helps me, because the handwriting is difficult to read. This is what he wrote:

11th January 1916

I can write now. But still can't work.

Father has to get along all by himself. I think he wants to leave.

Where could we go to?

I cannot write down what happened. I will bury it forever deep inside me. But the faces of the boys I will always have in front of me. And those of all the others, for whom we have become enemies. They claim father is a spy because of his platform! Despite the fact that he had left Germany because he didn't want to have anything to do with the German Reich or the Emperor!

Hillary has come and visited me. She stayed true to me, although everybody else is against us. Her mother has saved me. She came every day to see for my wounds. If it hadn't been for her, I think Mother wouldn't have been able to stand all this.

May be none of us.

She even makes the girls laugh.

Now the paradise definitely has become hell.

What in the world has happened to him/to them?
Did they beat him up? Search for clues, Henni!
Maybe Gilly Kneebone has written a letter to the
newspaper or somebody about what happened. Or has
other records than her day book?

Take care, Henni.

Leo

They beat him up and *burned* him?

They did something terrible . . . oh God, I wish I could turn off my imagination. And Leopold is right, where can they go? Anywhere in Australia they will be 'the enemy'. Hillary stays true, and Gilly is standing by them, but some think *she's* an anti-war nutcase, even people in her Day Book that she *nursed*! She got hate mail: 'Hun-lover', 'filthy traitor' – I've read the letters!

Gilly married a farmer. They had two children, Hillary and Joe. Gilly's husband was thrown from a horse and died. Hill never married. She lived in the bunga for most of her life. Helped the neighbours. Oh, there's so much *stuff*!

With a heavy heart, I'll search through Gilly's pile again.

What did they do to you, Leopold?

?g

Cauldron Bay, Sandy's, Thursday 8 December 6pm

I found this in an envelope, no address, in the back of Gilly's writing pad. I guess she didn't know where to send it.

I can't read it without crying.

Poor poor Leopold. What will become of you now?

I feel as if I know him but there's nothing I can do.

Oh, Soccerman, I'm sitting here with tears dripping from my chin. I never thought my friend would suffer like this.

so senseless and cruel

why?

sorry

taking Boz fo r a walk

Gilly Witness.jpg

Saturday, 2nd January, 1916

This afternoon at four O'clock I was called to the Schmidt house to attend to Leopold Schmidt. I was shocked by the sight that met my eyes and the story of its cause.

Earlier today Bruce Davis, Brian Davis, Thomas Black and Frank Howard, forced Leopold to climb naked to the top of a platform built in a tall gum tree by Leopold's father. They then taunted him. Finally they set fire to the ladder.

While scrambling down the burning ladder to save himself, Leopold sustained burns to his hands, arms, legs and particularly the soles of his feet.

The wounds will heal, but the hurt and humilition will not.

As a constant visitor to the Schmidt household, attending his mother for two years now, I have come to know Leopold. He is a cautious, orderly, well mannered young man and I know he would not have done anything to provoke this outrageous act. His german origin has been callously used against him. The sad fact is that the Schmidt family, who are peaceful decent people, came to Cauldron Bay believing it to be safe from the barbarism they saw growing around them in Berlin, before the war began.

I will stand witness to this cruel and cowardly act.

G Kneebone

Sorry, Soccerman, I'm okay. Feeling a bit stupid. In case Gilly's handwriting is hard for you to read, here's what she wrote.

Saturday, 2nd January, 1916

This afternoon at four o' clock I was called to the Schmidt house to attend to Leopold Schmidt.

I was shocked by the sight that met my eyes and the story of its cause.

Earlier today Bruce Davis, Brian Davis, Thomas Black and Frank Howard forced Leopold to climb naked to the top of a platform built in a tall gum tree by Leopold's father. They then taunted him. Finally they set fire to the ladder.

While scrambling down the burning ladder to save himself, Leopold sustained burns to his hands, arms, legs and particularly the soles of his feet. The wounds will heal, but the hurt and humiliation will not.

As a constant visitor to the Schmidt household, attending his mother for two years now, I have come to know Leopold. He is a cautious, orderly, well mannered young man and I know he would not have done anything to provoke this outrageous act. His German origin has been callously used against him. The sad fact is that the Schmidt family, who are peaceful decent people, came to Cauldron Bay

believing it to be safe from the barbarism they saw
growing around them in Berlin, before the war began.

I will stand witness to this cruel and cowardly act.
G Kneebone

I know it happened back then and the world has turned, and the years have gone by, but they were so *cruel*! *Why?*

All I can think is that it was such a desperately sad time in Cauldron Bay that everyone wanted to blame someone, so they blamed the Schmidts. (I think blaming makes you feel better. Feels like you have a reason.) Only the Kneebones could still see the Schmidts as real people. I guess the Davises and the others pointed to the platform, and saw Konrad with his binoculars, and didn't *want* to believe he was simply watching birds.

'What a sad state of affairs,' as Mrs Biddle would say.

Why can't we accept people who aren't exactly like us – like Leopold? Like Felix?

Do we *all* have to be the *same* before the world can be peaceful?

And another thing I've thought about – understanding language. If you couldn't translate Leopold's writing we wouldn't know *any* of this. It would just be gobbledygonk or whatever the word is.

And I wouldn't be miserable.

But I'm glad you did.

H

Mensch, Henni, don't think you are a fool.

Because you aren't.

Not a bit.

I had to swallow hard when I read Gilly Kneebone's statement. It's not only history.

Not long ago, in a village about a hundred kilometers north of Berlin, a group of boys age 16 beat another boy to death because he had his hair dyed red and wore an earring and belonged to a group of left activists (the Neo-Nazis call them "ticks"). Then they threw his body into a pit with liquid manure.

Makes me shiver.

Do you think the Cauldron Bay people of today know what the boys did to Leopold and that's why they behave so strangely? To cover up what those boys did?

But why? After all, it is history. Those who live today didn't do it.

The answer must be in the papers Konrad hid. Somehow they must be connected with today.

The platform?

Remember the tower in Ting Tang Tellerlein?

At the platform is there a place where you could hide papers safely? Have you been onto the platform when you were in Cauldron Bay?

I will ask Felix, the riddle boy, if he's got an idea. And we'll go over to Sascha's place

232

and ask him to show us his video of Cauldron Bay again. When we see the place it might give us a clue. Who knows?

Omi called and said this Ting Tang Tellerlein sounds very familiar. She is sure the words belong to a hopping game little girls used to play. But she didn't remember more lines than those we already know. She promised to ask a friend and call me back tomorrow.

Got to pick up Lotte. And prepare the evening meal. Parents will be home late. I'll check my inbox before I go to bed.

I have always thought the phrase "my thoughts will be with you" sounds silly. But just now it feels right to say: mine truly are with you.

Leo

Quick email. Mick's doing the weather readings. No, I don't think Mick knows what happened to Leopold, but he's scared of something. He wants me to go home, which makes him even more angry at the pump!

He had another go at me last night. 'You know this is none of your business. (As if the past belongs to the relatives of the dead!) They were different times. You have no idea what was going on.'

Neither does he, and he doesn't want to know.

I can't go to the platform today. Have to help Mrs Biddle clean out the big fridge – punishment for all the riding off and not telling what's going on. But I can't. I don't *know* what's going on.

Last Easter I did climb up to the platform. Terrifying! Especially scrambling on and off, because it's just a flat platform about twenty metres up a giant gum, with no rails!

The climbing ladder we used has gone. There's no place to hide anything up there. If Konrad wanted Leo or Bettina to find the papers, he wouldn't put them up there.

BIG DEVELOPMENT!
Remember I wrote to the Aboriginal galleries and got a reply? Well, the Living Link to Leopold rang home!! The Gerit!!! Remember? Mum called here early before she went to work. Left a message. She woke everyone up.

Mick went mad! 'This place doesn't revolve around you, Miss Octon. You might behave like this in the city but not here. We're doing you a favour and don't you forget it.'

Felt like moving to Sandy's.

It's so weird. School will be going on back home and I'm still here.

Craig's hanging around like a dog waiting its chance.
He shoved a stick under my nose with a spider. He goes, 'White tail. One bite – amputation!'

Please solve that riddle – yes, Felix, Sascha, Bettina, all the brains on the job. I don't know how long I'm going to last here.
I might be dropped at the bus stop any time, the way Mick is.

Soon as I can tomorrow I'll go to the platform, to search round the base.

Someone's coming

H

Berlin, Donnerstag 8.Dezember 23.46

Okay, you go to the platform and I'll be on
my computer Saturday morning at six (my time),
which will be four in the afternoon in Cauldron
Bay. Felix will join me — he is going to stay
overnight at my place.

We will stay there as long as necessary.

I told Mustafa what was going on and he
said if I don't show up for the match in the
afternoon, he will find an excuse for me and
score a goal for you!

Leo

The platform looked so sinister up against the grey sky. I tried not to think of Leopold, and reminded myself it had been lucky for us last Easter. I was wading through bushes at the base of the tree thinking, Who is hiding in this tower? Who is hiding in this tower? and holding back a branch so I could take a step when I saw a burnt stick on the ground in front of me. Then it moved.

It was a *tiger snake!*

It was gone in a flash, but I had to sit on a fallen log till my heart stopped pounding and my legs would obey me again. I tell you Leo, it was hard to keep looking! I crashed around and told myself the snake would be as scared as I was. Couldn't see any sign of . . . rocks? stones? papers? I looked on the trunk, in the ferns, on trees nearby . . . I felt scared and frustrated. What am I looking for, Leo?

Then, when I stopped to pick burrs out of my socks, I noticed other crackling noises stopped too! I couldn't see anything. I went on. The noises went on!

An animal? But an animal wouldn't stop like that.

Someone was there!

Then there was an ear-splitting *CRACK!* Maybe it was a gunshot, maybe it was a branch . . . I was *terrified!*

I bolted back towards the house, getting scratched and prickled, but the path looked different so I ran another way. Then the bush got thicker and the ground steeper and I knew it was wrong. I turned around to go back but I'd totally lost my bearings! I was praying to God, I tell you.

Then, through a gap in the tree tops, I saw the platform. Struggling to keep it in view and trying not to panic I scrambled through the bush back to the tree. I found the right way, stumbled down to the Schmidts' house and raced down the track to my bike.

It wasn' t there!!!

Someone had thrown it in the ferns on the other side of the road.

I'm at Sandy's.

With Boz.

It's too scary.

I don't know what I'm looking for, Leo.

It's too hard.

Are you there?

DON'T GIVE UP, HENNI!
WE'VE GOT IT!

After we've read your mail with pounding hearts (well, for my part anyway), Felix pushed me aside, saying, "How stupid can one be," googled "Ting Tang Tellerlein" — and POP! there it was, even two versions of the whole thing.

First version:

Ting Tang Tellerlein,
Wer klopft an meine Tür?
Ein wunderschönes Mägdelein,
das sprach zu mir:
Erster Stein, zweiter Stein, dritter Stein soll
    bei mir sein —
eins — zwei — drei

Ting Tang Little Plate
Who is knocking at my door?
A beautiful maiden
Who said to me:
First stone, second stone, third stone
    should be with me –
One – two – three.

The second version:

> *Ting Tang Tellerlein!*
> *Wer sitzt in diesem Turm?*
> *Des Königs schönes Töchterlein*
> *Und das sprach so:*
> *Brecht einen Stein,*
> *Den zweiten Stein,*
> *Den dritten Stein,*
> *Damit ich kann befreiet sein!*

> **Ting Tang Little Plate!**
> **Who is sitting in this tower?**
> **The king's beautiful daughter**
> **who spoke thus:**
> **Break one stone,**
> **the second stone,**
> **the third stone,**
> **so I can be freed!**

Who is the beautiful maiden or the king's
daughter? Someone precious? Something precious?
A treasure? Gold?

    BUT more important: Both have the third stone!

We saw stone steps on the Cauldron Bay DVD
last night. We have been watching it over again.

    Do you get me?

    The stone steps leading up to Konrad's house.
The papers could be underneath the third stone.
From the top, we would guess. But could be from
the bottom. Just go there and try.

    Give it one last go.

    Leo and Felix

Cauldron Bay, Sandy's, Saturday 10 December 4.45pm

I don't want to go back!
I'm scared.
Third stone – sounds right though
well
we have to know

Okay

Should take an hour, roughly, unless something happens

Here goes nothing

I FOUND IT!!
THIRD STEP FROM THE TOP!!!
A BISCUIT TIN!

I'm at Sandy's. I've locked the door. I told Mrs Biddle I was going for a walk along the beach.   Tea soon. Must hurry.

All the steps rest on big rocks except for *the third step from the top!* It's on smaller rocks. I levered out the middle stone to find a little dry cave – and there it was!
A waterproof pouch – like something a sailor would use – and inside it a German biscuit tin, and inside a bag with a receipt and a letter signed by Konrad.
   Leo, the Biddles don't own the land the store is on!

Someone's outside! What should I do?
The receipt is from George Biddle. It says: To Konrad Schmidt for purchase of fifteen acres of land in Main Street, Cauldron Bay. Payment received 120 pounds/£120.
   Konrad's English isn't great but the message is very clear. He says they are leaving Cauldron Bay and although he paid the money to George, the land is still not in his name. The Transfer of Title has not been completed.
   Boz is growling!! I have the bike inside.
   Leo, the legal stuff wasn't done!!
   What about Mrs Biddle? The store has been her home for so long *but the land isn't theirs!*
   What should I do?
   Leave the papers here?

Henni — did anyone see you get the papers?
Anyway, the proof is there now. The land belongs
to the Schmidts.

Pretty smart, that Konrad!

Felix and I have talked it over.

The land must go back to its owner. It was
stolen from the Schmidts and we don't think
the Biddles should profit from that theft, even
though they personally did not steal it.

But on the other hand, can land really be
owned? Shouldn't it just be lived on?

Then it would be the Biddles who should stay
on it?

We think it is best you talk to Mrs Biddle
about it. She seems to be someone who is able to
listen. And she is not in the same way involved
as Mick — she is not from Cauldron Bay, true?

Leo + Felix

Cauldron Bay, Sandy's, Saturday 10 December 6.30pm

Leo, I'm off!

If you don't hear from me in 4 hours call my mother.
03 9744 5698 – don't know what code from Germany.

Berlin, Sonnabend, 10.Dezember 12.32

Henni. The four hours are over. We haven't heard from you.

Shall we call your mother? L + F

Berlin, Sonnabend, 10.Dezember 12.41

H E N N I ? ? ? ? ? ? ? ?

Berlin, Sonnabend, 10.Dezember 12.53

I called your mother. Boy, that was strange.
She first thought I was joking, then she was
alarmed. So are we. Where are you?

Now what?

We'll stay on the computer.

Please, let us know what happened.

Leo + Felix

Leo loves Henni!

Berlin, Sonnabend, 10.Dezember 12.54

D A N I E L LE !!!!! GET OFF !!!!!!

Cauldron Bay, Biddles', Saturday 10 December 10.55pm

Mum called
I'm okay
But oh boy BIG SHOWDONW!
And you'll never guess who's here –
LivingLink to Leopold!
allgood
tell you soon as I can

H

Berlin, Sonntag, 11.Dezember 15.39

Fine, you are okay, but what about me???

Did you dump me?

If you don't tell me what happened I'll drop dead eaten up by curiosity!

You know the Xmas holidays begin soon. Well, within two weeks.

But then I'll be away. And there is no internet, no nothing. It's just a hut in the mountains.

So *plea-ease* let me know what happened.

I am dying!

Leo

Sorry Leo! Things just kept happening. It's a wild story.
But now I'll tell it properly, so get comfortable!

When I left Sandy's, I shoved the tin of papers in my jacket
and rode for my life, bumping and bouncing on the dirt road,
pedalling like fury. Then a motorbike roared up behind me!
I knew it was Dreadful Greg. He gunned the engine till it
screamed, then as he roared past he stuck out his foot, but
I hit a sandy patch!! He missed me because my bike slewed!
I was still upright, but a handlebar dug into my side – *OWW!!
it killed!!!!!!!* I pounded on, heart thumping, legs burning,
terrified he was waiting for me up ahead.

Phew!! I made the store. Walking up the steps with jelly
legs was hard and my left side – *agony!!* but worst of all was
the truth in my jacket. I slipped into my room. Mrs Biddle was
stacking something, thank goodness.

Tea that night was chops. Not neat ones like you get in the
supermarket, but chunky rough-cut chops with carrots and
potatoes and Mrs Biddle's tomato sauce in a beer bottle, which
came out – *Blop!* – onto the edge of my plate and my jumper.

I was wrecked. Mick and Craig ignored me, gnawing their
chop bones like wild animals. Mrs Biddle tried to calm things
down. We were sitting at Konrad's table, in the place which
should have been the Schmidts' happy future. I didn't know if
Craig was involved with Dreadful Greg. And if I leaned to the
left – *Ooww! Torture!* I tell you, Soccerman, I was miserybags.
When Mrs Biddle said, 'We'll take you to the bus tomorrow,'
I mumbled, 'Thank you.'

Then came the squeak-*bang* of the door as someone walked

into the shop. Mrs Biddle went out to serve. Then I heard my name and Mrs Biddle said, 'Well, you'd better come in then.'

Through the door, following Mrs Biddle, strode a woman in jeans, boots and a worn heavy jacket. She had thick grey hair twisted up on her head. We all stood up.

Mrs Biddle said, 'This is Henni.'

The woman stepped towards me. 'Hello Henni, I'm Gerit, Leopold Schmidt's grand-daughter.'

I flopped down onto my chair. The Living Link had just walked in!!!!!!!

Mrs Biddle said slowly, 'I think we should all sit down.'

Mess*MessMESS*!!!! *Mess* of Dreadful Greg and Craig. *Mess* of greasy bones and tomato sauce. *Mess* of my aching side. *Mess* of the past burst into the present. *MESS OF LIVES!*

Mick gave me a glare like a storm cloud that said, Get *rid* of her!

'I rang your mum, Henni,' said Gerit, unconcerned. 'I told her not to tell you I was coming in case I didn't make it. I've just driven down from Alice Springs. I thought it's only another day's drive, I'll keep moving.'

'Have you had any tea?' Mrs Biddle asked in a welcoming way.

'Yes, thanks, but I'd love a coffee.' Gerit was quiet, but not shy. 'That coast road's a beauty! I'm used to roads that go straight for a hundred k. This all feels like a bit of a dream.'

She was dreaming! *My* head floated like a bubble. What was I going to *say*?

Then they were talking about the weather station.

Finally it came. 'So Henni, what have you found out about my grandfather?'

'Did you know him?' I bleated.

'Oh yes, very well. He looked after me a lot when I was a kid.

He died when I was twenty-seven, and you know something, he never mentioned this place. Never.'

Of course he didn't. It was *hell* for him.

Suddenly my voice was strong! Leopold's story was so fresh in my mind. I told it as if it had happened to my friend just yesterday, I told her about the Schmidts' move to Australia, which began with such hope, and Konrad building the wooden house, and the platform high in a tree. And then the war.

'Now *just hold on a minute!*' growled Mick, slamming his hands on the table. 'This is your imagination running wild on fourth-hand hearsay.' He nodded to Gerit. 'Sorry to break it to you like this, lady, but Konrad Schmidt was a spy. He built that platform to spy for the Germans.'

'He did *not*!' I shouted.

Mick ignored me. 'Australia was directly under threat. The Germans were established in the Pacific. They had a permanent cruiser squadron on the coast of China. They had Kaiser-Wilhelmsland up the north-east of New Guinea and they were empire building! You don't know what it was like at the time. They were going to bombard Perth and cut off the supply lines. We could've all been speaking German.'

'But even if he was spying for the Germans, which he *wasn't*, how would he ever get the news to their navy from here?' I cried.

'Pigeon, messenger – they have ways. Gilly Kneebone, she got around, she had crazy ideas.'

'But you don't *know*!' I protested.

'I know a darn sight better than *you*,' thumped Mick.

'Why would he spy if they left Germany to get *away* from all that?' I said.

'That's your fancy ideas.' Mick glared at me. 'Why else would they come here? They were rich. They arrived with all the trappings. The little girl got a beautiful rocking horse for her birthday. No kid round here ever had a toy like that. You'd be lucky if you got a stick with a jam tin for a head and a hank of rope for a tail. Everyone knows the story of that rocking horse. Why else would they come here?'

It was Craig's smirk that did it.

As I felt for the tin at the back of the wardrobe a voice in my head was screaming, *What are you doing to the Biddles?*

But another voice was saying, The Schmidts were betrayed by so many people. *Am I going to betray them too?*

I put the tin on the table.

'What's this?' goes Mick.

I took a deep breath. First I told them about you – the boy in Berlin. (I sure wasn't going to tell them your name was Leo Schmidt – they were having enough trouble believing what I said!) They remembered Sascha, and they knew I had boxes from under the house. Well, Gerit didn't – she sat listening with eyes like saucers.

Then I told them about the trunk at Sandy's, and Gilly Kneebone's Day Book, and Leopold's diary in German, which the boy in Berlin translated, and finally Gilly's witness letter about Leopold and the fire.

Gerit was sniffing, searching in her pockets, till Mrs Biddle passed her a roll of toilet paper and she gave her nose a mighty blow.

Then I told them how the boy in Berlin found the clue in *Ting Tang Tellerlein* and I had searched round the platform (Craig was studying his boot! *bloody Craig!!!!!*), then finally how I found this tin under the third step.

Everyone stared at the tin.

Gerit drew it towards her. Carefully her long bony fingers took off the lid. I was shaking and biting my lip to keep from crying. I thought of Konrad wrapping it up for Leopold to find. Sorry Konrad, it missed two generations.

Gerit unfolded the papers as if she was unfolding time.

Then she read them out. When she began to read about the land sale, the only sounds were the wind in the trees and the crack and hiss of the fire in the stove.

You would not *believe* the electricity in that room.

Silence.

Then Mick gave a deep sigh. 'So, as I understand it, Grandpop Biddle sold Konrad the paddock, took his money, but never got the legals straight.'

Suddenly Craig leapt up and grabbed the documents. 'I'll burn 'em. There goes your proof!' and he rushed to the stove.

Mick roared, '*Craig! Give me that!*' He snatched the papers in a rage and slammed them on the table. He stormed across the kitchen and leaned on the sink. I could see the huge muscles in his arms. Then he picked up a glass. He was going to say something but instead he held the glass under the tap. Then he wrenched the tap on *hard*. The jet of water hit the bottom of the glass and shot up higher than his head, but he stood there. Nobody moved. Water shooting everywhere, cascading, pouring, *streaming* down. Then slowly he turned off the tap, walked back and thrust the papers at Gerit. 'Stop this nonsense once and for all,' he growled. 'What do you want us to do?'

Gerit stood up slowly and took the documents. She looked at saturated Mick, and us, and around the flooded kitchen for a long, long moment then she laid the documents on the table.

'These papers belong in a museum,' she said quietly. 'I didn't come here to claim anything. I don't need this place.

I came here to find out about my grandfather. He was a hard man to live with.'

'Oh, Lordy Lord,' said Mrs Biddle, shaking her head.

A door banged. We all jumped.

'Storm coming,' said Craig.

'I think it just passed,' said Gerit simply.

Mick had cooled down. He slumped in a chair, a sorry sight; soaking, crumpled, thinning wet hair plastered over his forehead. 'You know, all my life I felt there was something they never told about this place, something fishy, but Dad never took me seriously.' Mick shrugged. 'What could I've done anyway? But they should've told me.'

'Who'd like a beer?' said Mrs Biddle, tossing him a towel and starting to mop up.

'Me,' I said.

'You're too young,' laughed Gerit.

Then the phone rang. It was Mum. 'The boy in Berlin is asking about you.'

'There's that boy in Berlin again!' said Gerit.

'Email him now,' said Mick.

So, Leo, I did.

Told you it would be long. And there's more. Not now though.

Ooooo – an *itchy* bit! I have heaps of scabs!! Broose is navy-purple with a tinge of yellow like a storm cloud. Mum said I was dead lucky I didn't crack a rib.

What's happening in Berlin? Is Christmas still coming?

Hello Felix!

Read you.

H

Berlin, Montag, 12.Dezember 16.50

Boy, what a messy story! All that tomato sauce
makes me think of a bad movie full of blood!!!
I was reading it like a detective story, only
with much more suspension.

Gee, I wouldn't have wanted to be in your skin.

Felix is slumped on my bed, watching me type.
We think it's good how it turned out. If Gerit
doesn't need the land for her life, it's fair, the
Biddles can stay. After all, they were not the
ones who forced the Schmidts out of Cauldron Bay
and it was Mick's grandparents who kept the land,
knowing that it belonged to the Schmidts. Although
on the other hand — Mick's family has profited all
their lives from the fact that they have inherited
that "stolen" land, and Mick suspected something,
right? Bettina says: The best thing is, that
the truth came out and will stay alive, when the
papers will be shown in a museum.

And all this happened only because you didn't
do what people always say: Don't stick your nose
into other people's business; past is past, don't
touch it.

I am so happy that nothing happened to you.
In the time between my phone call and your
email I bit my nails off to where you can't bite
anymore. Felix was chewing his collar again. What
a relief when your mail popped up! But did you
find out what happened to the Schmidts? We are
waiting for the sequel.

It's not five o'clock yet but it's already dark outside. Across the street people have Xmas decoration in the windows. Lights all over.

Lotte is counting the days till Xmas. She has a calendar where you open a little window every day and you find a piece of chocolate and a picture. She is waiting for the presents Santa Claus (Weihnachtsmann in German = Christmasman) will bring. I tease her and say there is no Santa Claus, then she gives me this look, like, can't you count till three? (meaning: are you stupid?) and says: "And who brings the presents? You won't get anything, if you don't believe in him." Then I make a real serious face and say: "Who needs presents anyway?" Then she howls and throws herself against me. And then she stops and grins and says: "I know the parents bring the presents, but I like Santa Claus!"

Bettina and Lotte are baking Xmas cookies.

Oh, one more thing. Felix has been bugging me to send you this riddle, which I didn't do because I thought you had enough riddles to solve. Here it is. And I tell you, the solution is fascinating.

★   ★   ★

Okay: you have nine
dots (well, stars,
because it's Xmas).   ★   ★   ★

★   ★   ★

How can you connect them all with no more than
four straight lines, without taking the pencil
off?

Boy, the cookies are calling! Zimtsterne
(cinnamonstars) are my favorite. I think we need
to check the kitchen, see if they do everything
right! Bye, Henni

L

+

F

I'm giving Danielle a Tavla board for Christmas. It sounds *exactly* her kind of game. Hopping and noisy. Those stars from Felix are in my head. But before Cauldron Bay becomes history, well, some of it *is* history, I want to tell you the rest. It will be like a long letter or a diary. *Another* diary!

Okay, so after the big scene in the kitchen we all went to bed, and that night in Cauldron we got 'a bit of a blow', which is how the Biddles describe a gale. But Gerit slept in her swag, beside her old station wagon. Next morning early, she woke me up with a *tap tap* on the window, and beckoned, Come to the beach?

ooouww!!!! The Broose! Somehow I got my shoes on . . .

The wind had blown strips of bark all over the road. I wondered if Gerit would feel the thrill of bursting out of the tea-tree at the top of the dune with the sea stretched out and the sky so huge.

She did! She leaned into the wind and took it in. '*Wow!* I can see why Konrad loved this place.'

By now the sun was a line of gold on the horizon, beneath a blanket of grey cloud, then – and it's just as well you weren't here for this bit, Leo – Gerit *stripped off* and hurtled down the dune and into the sea!!!! Dived straight into a huge wave!

I stood there pleading – *Please God, please don' t let her get taken by a rip!*

She took a couple of strokes and then – *Oh, thank you, thank you!* – she came out as fast as she went in.

I didn't know where to look. The Living Link naked!!!!!

'*Whoow!*' she said, drying herself furiously with her scarf. 'I'm tingling! Wonderful!'

261

It's funny, because you know, Soccerman, that's *exactly* what we did when we first saw Cauldron Bay at Easter, except it was sunny and we all ran in with our clothes on.

Gerit and I walked along the beach, our eyes watering from the wind. You should have been there for this bit, Leo. It was embarrassing, all the stuff she said about how much this meant to her. Were your ears burning? She wanted to know how we emailed each other, how the translations worked.

She said, 'I can understand my Grandpa's bitterness now. He trusted very few people. And he sure taught my mother to think for herself. Every generation leaves its stamp on the next. Grandpa sure influenced me.'

'Did your grandfather have any scars?' I asked.

'You mean on his body?' She gave a long sigh. 'Yes. The left side of his face was normal, handsome in fact, but the right side . . .' She shook her head. 'It was cruel.'

'His *face*?' I exclaimed. 'But Gilly Kneebone just said his hands and feet.'

'The house fire.'

'*Another* fire?'

'When he lost his family.'

'*WHAT?*'

'Yes, he was the only one to survive.'

'*NO!*'

I felt faint.

'Nobody told you?' She put her arms around me. 'Come on, Henni. Let's get you to those rocks ahead.' She sort of scooped me to a sheltered spot out of the wind, where she rubbed my arms and shoulders and talked, and talked, and gradually I came to accept the idea that Konrad, Bettina, Gretel and Christa had all died in a fire.

'Come on, Henni, I know you've found out a lot about the Schmidt family and they've become real for you. And it feels like you've lost friends, but it was such a long time ago. I only found out when Mum researched it. It's history. You're more upset than I was.' Finally Gerit said, 'We need breakfast.'

The wind pushed us back down the beach and was the excuse for my red eyes.

'Mavis has whipped up a storm,' said Mick, pulling out chairs for us at the table.

Mrs Biddle sure had been busy. She'd sent Craig for homemade yoghurt from some relative with a dairy.

'Best yoghurt I've ever tasted,' said Gerit.

'I took you for a yoghurt person,' said Mrs Biddle, really pleased.

There was a choice of six cereals, four jams (the best stuff from the shop), and bacon and scrambled eggs, and tomatoes and mushrooms and homemade bread (from the yoghurt relative). The big surprise was the table. They'd taken off the heavy plastic tablecloth and it was set with mats. For the first time you could actually see the wood. It was a beautiful deep rich honey colour.

'How long can you stay?' Mrs Biddle asked Gerit.

'I'll head back to Melbourne early this afternoon. Want a lift, Henni?'

'*Yes!*'

Then Mick stood up and gave a little speech, which really surprised me. It sounded rehearsed but sincere.

'Henni, I'm sorry. You were right. What happened to the Schmidts was a bloody disgrace.' Then he turned to Gerit. 'And we're very moved by your generosity, Gerit, and we'd like you to

263

have this table, which is one of Konrad's.'

Mrs Biddle was sitting there hitching her straps and beaming.

'Mum always said it was too good for us,' said Craig.

'Thank you,' said Gerit. She ran her hand over the wood. 'I'll treasure it. You've taken such good care of it.'

'I'll help you tie it on your roof-rack,' said Craig.

'Finish your breakfast first,' said Mrs Biddle.

I rang Sandy to ask if I could show Gerit the trunk and the bunga.

'Sure,' said Sandy. 'My parents are home. They want to meet you.'

We all crowded into the bunga. Sandy's dad knew a fair bit about Hillary. 'Leopold was the love of her life,' he said simply. 'She never married, which was tragic because she was great with kids. Practically raised the three Gibson boys when their mother was ill and their father away shearing. But no one ever measured up to Leopold.'

'Why didn't Leopold come back to Hillary?' I asked.

'Don't know. Well, it probably took him some time to recover from the burns,' said Sandy's dad, 'then what did he have to offer her? There's an article about that fire somewhere . . .' He began searching through a bundle of old newspaper clippings.

Gerit held Leopold's diary as if it was a butterfly that might fly away at any moment. She studied Gilly's Day Book and letter of witness, then there was talk about who should have the different documents.

'I found it!' Sandy's dad waved a newpaper article. 'I'll give you a copy, Henni.'

When he handed it to me I put it in my pocket. I couldn't read it then.

Gerit is keeping Leopold's diary. She knows someone who can translate it, so you've lost that job, Leo. And I'm attaching the newspaper report. I'm warning you, it's sad.

I took Gerit to the Schmidts' house and showed her where I found the tin, then we leaned on the verandah rail and looked out at the trees.

'Are you going to buy the house?' I asked her.

'No, I'm not a house person,' she said. 'Besides, I haven't got the money. You buy it.'

'No. Even if I was a millionaire I wouldn't buy it. It's too sad.'

'Come on, Henni, it was a long time ago. You had a great holiday here.'

'I'm in mourning.'

Then we crashed through the bush up to the platform. Now, Soccerman, this will amaze you. When Gerit saw it, she *laughed like a kid!!*

'I pricked up my ears when I heard Konrad had a platform,' she said. 'And sure enough it's a *shloop*! Grandpa built a *shloop* in a tree at home, but not nearly so high.'

'A *shloop*?' I asked.

'Well, my family built them, and that's what they called them. It's like a cubby, a place to sit, where you can think, dream, whatever . . . where the world looks beautiful . . .'

'How did he get up there?' I asked. 'We couldn't figure it out.'

'He shot a slingshot over the branch with a light line attached, which pulled up a strong rope, which pulled up a ladder. Or sometimes he did the monkey trick. You need strong boots for it, but it's not hard. I'll show you some time.'

'Do you have a *shloop*?'

'Not up a tree. It's a stump overlooking Ormiston Pound near Alice Springs. Maybe one day I'll show you. Do you have a *shloop*?'

'Well, there's a rock where I watch the waves.'

(I liked the way she said, 'I'll show you sometime.')

Still awake, Soccerman?

Meanwhile back at the store, as they say, Mick and Craig had the table on the roof-rack, all wrapped up and tied down tight.

Mick said, 'It's going to rain. You should get going. Not wanting to get rid of you or anything, but you know that road.'

I said to Mick, 'Remember what you said about me imagining Leopold? Well, I think you were right.'

'We were all a bit right and a lot wrong,' said Mick. 'Only one who wasn't is this one,' and he grabbed Mrs Biddle and gave her a kiss. 'Isn't she a beaut?'

'Oh, get away with you,' laughed Mrs Biddle.

We said our goodbyes, which felt pathetic considering everything, and Craig, who was kicking stones, nearly looked at me when we shook hands! I wished him luck finding extra-poisonous things that can kill you even faster.

Mrs Biddle gave us a box of lunch (half the shop!) and we set off.

It was a sad journey. A light mist began to fall halfway along the coast road. We saw grey strings of birds over the water. Then the rain got heavier and the wind dropped. The steady rhythm of the windscreen wipers as they swept away the rain felt like part of my mourning for the Schmidts, for Leopold, as if they were wiping away my tears as we drove away from Cauldron Bay.

Gerit and I would talk about something for a while, then we'd travel along thinking about it.

'Why were you so curious about the Schmidts?' Gerit asked.

I'd thought about this a lot.

'We loved their house. They were a mystery. I felt I knew Leopold – not like a ghost or anything – but as a boy my own age. I felt alone in Cauldron Bay, and I imagined him feeling alone too, like me. I turned him into a friend.'

Then it was my turn. 'Why did you drive all the way to Cauldron Bay, so suddenly?'

'Well,' said Gerit, 'I was travelling south anyway, and as I covered the k's I kept remembering Grandpa. I thought here's a chance to find out about his childhood. I loved that old bloke. He smelt of pipe tobacco and Solvol, a sort of hard soap we used to use. He was a moody bugger, and strict, but he always had time for me, always wanted to know what I'd been doing, and included me in his plans.' She laughed. 'Two old German men and Gerit go fishing, three old German men and Gerit play Skat on the back veranda, Grandpa and Gerit. Suited Mum fine, although his whistling drove her mad, and she thought he was too fond of red wine. Which he probably was.'

'Who did Leopold marry? Who was your Grandma?'

'Iris. Don't know much about her, just that she was a farm girl. She died before I was born. They only had the one child, my mum. Grandpa lived with us for as long as I can remember.'

'Did he like to read?'

'Oh yes, everything. I remember one of his favourites was "The Buln-Buln and the Brolga."'

'You said he had a strong influence on you. How?'

'Am I being paid for this interview?' she laughed. 'Well, for one thing he always took me with him when he went walkabout.'

'Walkabout?'

'Camping in the bush. And he never cared if I missed school. He knew all the birds and animals and plants, great teacher – and he had many Aboriginal friends, which probably set me on the path to what I do now.'

'What do you do, Gerit?'

'I have a rare job. I drive up to Central Australia, where I know the Aboriginal artists, and I'm sort of a go-between for the galleries in the cities and the artists and the Aboriginal art centres. It's pretty rough, but it's very rewarding. I've got a wonderful collection in the back right now. It'll be a great exhibition.'

'What, those boxes behind us in the back?'

'Yeah. That's why I was a bit twitchy when that bloke with the tatts came prowling round last night. Do you know him? What's his problem?'

'That's Greg Davis. He tried to knock me off the bike. Mrs Biddle calls him a "dreadful man". Weren't you scared?'

'Yeah, but I asked him what he was doing and I think I gave him the shock of his life. He said, "Checking." I said, "Everything's okay." Then, off in the distance, he and Craig had a blue. A lot of swearing. I don't know what that was about.'

'I think Craig's so used to being told what to do he can't decide for himself.'

'He needs to get away,' said Gerit.

'That's what Mrs Biddle says. Away from Greg.'

'Well, after last night I don't think there's much friendship left.'

Mrs Biddle's lunch, a stretch of our legs, and on we go.

Still raining.

'Did Leopold believe in God?' I asked.

'Would *you* believe in God after what he'd been through? No. He called religion "claptrap". He thought everyone should grow up and stand on their own two feet.'

'Do you believe in God, Gerit?'

She said, 'I think the idea of God has been belittled. Devalued. Oh my God! Thank God! God help us? God Almighty? There are many beautiful things to wonder at. Is that God? I don't know.'

'Where will you put the table?' I asked.

'Good question. My flat's tiny. I'll probably store it in a friend's garage.'

'Then why did you accept it?'

She paused. 'Because it was the right thing to do.' She thought for a second. 'Grandpa's diary is what's precious to me.'

'Gerit, I could look after the table. I have a table for my computer but there's not enough room for papers and books and other stuff at the side.'

'It's yours.'

We arrived home and life instantly became normal.

I'm attaching the newspaper article about the second fire. Read it when you're feeling strong.

H

fire claims 4.jpg

not have fallen between—
and the platform.

FIRE CLAIMS FOUR LIVES

ARARAT BLAZE

THREE DISQUIETING FEATURES.

Four lives were lost and one person critically injured in a house fire in McKinney Street, Ararat, on Monday at 3 a.m. Fanned by the strong north wind the flames spread with startling rapidity, and the building collapsed soon after the arrival of the fire brigade.

Considerable enquiry was needed to identify the deceased as their presence in the lodging, owned by Mr D Pearce, was unknown and all effects were burned. The sole survivor, Leopold Schmidt, aged 14, finally confirmed the deceased as Mr Konrad Schmidt, a cabinetmaker from Cauldron Bay, his wife Bettina and two daughters. Mr Schmidt, a German, was not registered with police in accordance with the Aliens' Restriction Order. It is believed, for this reason, they arrived at the lodging after dark, intending to rest before catching the train to Horsham next day. Mrs Schmidt was in ill health. The question of suspicious circumstances was raised and police are investigating.

The survivor of the fire effected escape by breaking a rear window. He is reported to have returned into the building in an attempt to rescue his sisters but was driven back by the flames. He sustained serious burns and was conveyed to Ararat's hospital most urgently by residents in Ararat's recently acquired Ashford Litter. Little hope is held for him.

Besides the suspicion of arson, there are two other disquieting features of the fire.

Councillor McPherson had previously reported unfavourably on Mr D Pearce's lodging, declaring it in a deplorable condition. Mr Pearce being away in Geelong could not reply. Secondly, this event bids us ask how many unregistered enemy aliens are moving among us?

FITZROY PATRIOTIC FUND

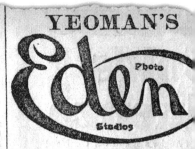

Hi Henni!
I am glad the story came to a good end. Your
story. But the Leopold story makes me sick —
I mean, how he lost his family. From one moment
to the other he was all by himself. In a strange
place. Not wanted. Maybe he wished he died too.
I would have, I think.

Bettina told me, around the time when I was
born, young right-wing Germans (the youngest was
16) set fire to a house where people from Turkey
lived, and two women and three children died.
The motive of the boys: they hated foreigners and
wanted them out. And that was not the only case.
It happened in many towns. It's frightening.
You're probably right. It's got to do with being
angry, unhappy, looking for somebody to blame.

Thanks for all the details, I lived every
single one. So it's all in dry towels now =
everything's worked out.

I am very familiar with the beast The Broose.

I don't know the word shloop. Bettina thinks
it could be "Schlupf" — the first part from the
word Schlupfwinkel = hiding place — or the second
part from Unterschlupf = hideout, cover. You
know what? I'll try to build such a shloop in the
trees where our Datsche is. Want to come up?

Today we had a new teacher, a substitute for the
Biology teacher who had a breakdown. Hope it

wasn't because of us. Anyway, we knew he was
coming and Maik prepared a nice surprise. On the
teacher's desk there is a plan with the name of
each student and a photo, in the order we are
sitting. Maik cut it up and reassembled it in a
new order. So now Felix was a blond girl, I was
a tall guy, Maik was Mustafa, and so on. We had
the greatest fun! Environmental adjustment.
We are discussing ecological systems now.

Antek has told his parents about his rock
performance at our school party. And you know
what his Dad did? He got out his old records —
real records, you know these big black discs with
grooves — and played them for Antek. All rock
music! And his mother tapped her foot with it!
"You think we were born as parents?" she said.
Not anymore!

Got to go, last meeting of the decoration group
before the big party. Maik is going to show me how
to do a tag. My tag. THE LION! (purring goodbye).

Hey, Henni, I am so happy, that you didn't
get bitten by all that poison that was around
you. We will survive!!! I'll turn on my CD
player (Bettina is not home!) and dan ... do my
homework.

Tschü-hüs! Leo

Felix tells you if you want to solve the riddle
with the nine stars you should try to think
beyond the given pattern.

Melbourne, Friday 16 December 4.37pm

Hello Soccerman!

We've just come back from lying around on picnic rugs in the park near our place – pizzas from The Upper Crust, with Zev and his parents, Tibor and Sue. Danielle whacked tennis balls into an oak trying to get the tree to catch them. Dad was hilarious.

'So Bernie climbs onto his desk like this,' goes Dad, telling about his new assistant, who skydives, 'and he checks his gear, and prays, and touches his Elvis rhinestone, and kisses his wedding ring and dives,' and Dad skydives – straight onto Sue's passionfruit pavlova, which was covered by a tea towel.

'It was a *surprise*!' wailed Sue.

'Sure was!' said Dad. 'I thought it was a cushion.'

Pavlova is a mess of fruit and cream and meringue all piled on top of each other, but it's more of a mess when it's been skydived onto!

So, here I sit, with my feet are up (respectfully) on Konrad's table and my big glass of Tropical Crush because it's HOT, and I have *six glorious weeks of never-ending summer holidays!!!* Ohappiness*OjoyObliss*sOjoyOhappinessOjoy*OblissO*joy

I hope you did't mind that l o o o n g email, Soccerman.

Well, let's face it, who *else* could I tell?

Incidently, I got an email from Gerit, who says an old family friend told her that Leopold *did* go back to see Hillary but she was minding those three little boys and Leopold thought they were *her* children and didn't even go up and *speak* to her! It's too sad. I can't even think about it. Not now.

273

I have invented something:

Yesterday I was cleaning the shower recess. *YUK!!!* Curly hair! *Danielle!!!!* I got mad at her. (My hair was there too.) Then I had this inspiration!

Q: Why am I angry?

A: I am angry because I hate cleaning the shower recess, so I want to blame someone.

The Gilly Kneebone Test!

What do you think, Leo? Should I tell the United Nations?

Ah, Maik, the joker! So now you know what it's like to be tall! *HEY!* Tell Felix there should be a joker in chess! The Jester! Wouldn't it be *great*? He moves two hops with your eyes shut. Also tell him THOSE 9 STARS ARE DRIVING ME UP THE WALNUTS!!!!! I want to get a huge wide brush, wider than the riddle, and join them all with one stroke! Answer please.

Hope your party's good. Talking of old people's music, this afternoon Mr Molloy said, 'I need three volunteers to clean up the big music room after the teachers' party last night. Who volunteers? Henni, Athena and Shirley.'

(Shirley's a Vietnamese girl who came at the end of last term.)

Oh boy, there were streamers, balloons, disgusting drink and food stuff *everywhere!* (You teachers, this is a *disgrace!* You've all got *detention*!!)

The CD player was still out, so Shirley turned up 'Yellow Submarine' and was pop-popping balloons in time to the music, and Athena was winding me up in streamers like I was a maypole when Mr Molloy sticks his head in.

'Hey, you're *cleaning up* a party, not *having* a party!'

We three are going to the movies tomorrow night.

READY FOR A MIRACLE?   *Drrrrrrrrrrrrrrrrrrrrrrrrrrrrrrrum roll!*

Aidan gave a report on a rugby game!

And, believe it or not, it was detailed and funny. Rugby might be interesting after all! ('Oh yeah?' goes Danielle. She's sticking stars on her ceiling – her third galaxy!)

I missed the Shetland ponies because I was still in Cauldron. Athena said she did all the talking because Matisse has a sprained wrist. She got on the left side of the Shetland pony and fell off the right side – forgot to stop in the middle!

My talk was the last one. I stuck to Leopold's story. First I described the world in 1913, Mother England, baby Australia and Germany flexing its muscles, then life in Cauldron Bay when the foreign family arrived. I told about the house and how the Schmidts left suddenly. I drew their family tree on the board with big question marks. That's when I noticed how quiet everyone was.

I told about the interviews, well, you know the story. (About the translations I just said, 'I emailed a friend in Germany.') When the bell rang, I asked Miss Dakin if I should stop and everyone yelled *'No, no! What happened?'* And I finished up with Grandpa and Gerit. They clapped and clapped!!! Some kids stayed to ask questions. Archie wanted to talk about conscription. Miss Dakin was saying 'You must write it down, Henni.'

So Soccerman, it's over. It felt like shutting a book.

I'm so happy to be happy again. You know the best thing about my project?

You

Henni!!! Big news!!!!

But hold on! I don't want to fall with the door into the house — German for: blurt it straight out.

First, about handling the urge to blame — don't call the United Nations. Do what we do in street soccer. Somebody gets fouled or commits a foul, they raise their arm — then everybody stops and it's a free kick. So, you are free to kick Danielle!

Second I am going to show you the solution for the riddle.

Amazing? Just leave the given pattern and you find a new way!

N O W ! T H E B I G N E W S!

Sascha has been here for afternoon tea.

We lit the candles on our Advent wreath — Lotte had insisted on one, so Knut went with her to the park and collected fir-tree twigs. Then she made him buy a wooden ring, candle holders,

276

red candles and golden bells to do it properly.

Bettina put goodies on the table — like Stolle,
gingerbread, Dominosteine (chocolate-coated
cubes with gingerbread, jam, marzipan), Mandel-
Spekulatius (a good Xmas cookie with almonds) —
then she poured the tea.

And when we were all sitting and munching,
Sascha announced he had a present for me that
covered Xmas, Hanukkah, Chinese New Year, my
birthday, Easter, Mayday, Şeker Bayram, and every
other opportunity all in one. And he had to tell
me now because it included a decision of me and
the parents!

Big silence.

I kind of slid forward on my chair.

Big grin on Sascha's face (he loves to give
presents!) and then!

Da-da-daaah!

The present is:

An airline ticket to Australia, to Melbourne
that is. Sascha has to go there at Easter and
would take me!

If I wanted that is. And if the parents don't
object.

Boy, I certainly want to. Parents *have* to agree.

How about you, Henni?

Do you want me to come?

LeO???

About the authors

Elizabeth Honey is a popular, award-winning author of poetry, picture books and novels, including *45 & 47 Stella Street* and *The Ballad of Cauldron Bay*. She is also an artist and illustrates her own books. Elizabeth's books are published in many countries around the world.

Heike Brandt is a writer, translator and critic. She has always been passionate about children's literature, and she founded and ran a specialist children's bookstore in Berlin. Heike is the author of three books for young people: *Die Menschenrechte haben kein Geschlecht*, *Wie ein Vogel im Käfig* and *Katzensprünge*. She has translated over 70 books from English to German, including books from the UK, USA, Canada, Australia and Nigeria.

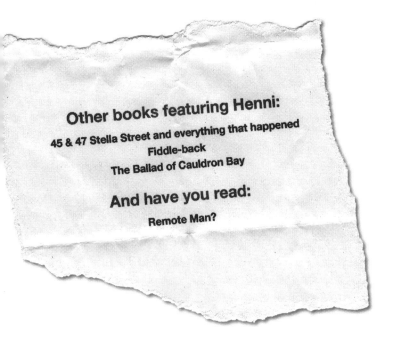

Other books featuring Henni:

45 & 47 Stella Street and everything that happened
Fiddle-back
The Ballad of Cauldron Bay

And have you read:

Remote Man?

How we wrote *To the Boy in Berlin*

Heike: When you translate somebody's books you get to know that person pretty well. Nobody reads a text more thoroughly than a translator. A translator has to create the story once again, in the words of her or his own language. I enjoyed Liz's way of looking at the world and telling stories about it. There were so many Australian expressions in her books: banana lounge? ute? witchetty grubs? I contacted Liz and got wonderful answers.

Elizabeth: I met Heike by fax, in 1997, when she was translating my story *45 & 47 Stella Street*. Years later, on holidays in Berlin with my family, we enjoyed a dinner at Heike's. My book *Remote Man* (containing email and chat) had been shortlisted for the German *Jugendliteraturpreis* that includes the translator too. I was curious about translations, the crazy German language and the relationship between the two countries. In 2003 I asked Heike if we could write a book together. The reply came back instantly. 'Yes.'

Heike: Liz asked me if I wanted to be a thirteen-year-old boy in her next book. Well, when I was thirteen I had wanted to be a boy (though now I am very happy to be a woman), so I agreed. I developed a character and a story in Berlin, and the ball started to roll.

Elizabeth: *Henni and Leo* was our working title. Heike sent the first email. Then she sent a second email changing one word. (*One word!* Since then whole sub-plots have gone!) Over the months, Henni and Leo exchanged emails. It was fun, but the plot rambled. Frustrated, I emailed, 'If we could just sit down and work on it together! Is there *any* way you could possibly come to Australia?' Heike wrote back, 'There is a translator's grant. I'm going for it.' I told my publisher, Rosalind Price, about this development. With her support and guidance I felt confident. And Heike got the grant.

Heike: When we went to Australia we had no idea what to expect. 'Just come,' we had been told. 'We'll see to the

279

rest.' And so it was. We felt welcome and at home, as if
we had been friends for ever. And then we started to work.
I was amazed at how firm and decided Liz was. She organised
and prepared, jotted down notes and plots, brought books and
background information and drew me in.

Elizabeth: Heike arrived in Melbourne In December 2005, and the
summer of Henni and Leo began. Working in Dame Nellie Melba
Kindergarten, we drew a large time line and marked on it German
and Australian holidays, German time, Australian time, and the
emerging pattern of emails. Like scriptwriters, we outlined our story on
cards – pink for Leo, aqua for Henni. Twice we presented our plot to the
publisher, who gave valuable criticism. After nearly three weeks, with
the plot done, Henni and Leo left the kinder.

Heike established a numbering system, e.g. 24 Leo #12, then we
began email ping-pong. The German visitors saw Canberra, Flinders,
Lorne, and Sydney, but wherever we were, Heike and I kept writing.
Sue Flockhart, our editor, met Heike too. Sue said meeting the author
is very helpful for the editing process.

Heike: As we were developing the story we got to know each
other's backgrounds, because we always had to explain why we
wanted this or that to happen, or not to happen. We thought
a lot, shared a lot, laughed a lot. So the process of writing
this book was a very enriching experience.

Elizabeth: By the time Heike flew home most emails were written,
but the polishing took more work. Finally, Rosalind and Sue read the
manuscript, and the contract was drawn up. Sue became keeper of
the 'hero' version, receiving our requests, e.g. 'Please replace existing
58 Henni #35.doc with this new one', then Leo's response would be
fine-tuned. Once again, much text was cut.

Heike: The publisher and editor always supported us in a very
positive way. They were encouraging, and at the same time
pointed out the flaws in our stories. It was a very trustful
and cooperative way of working together. In German I would
say: 'We all pulled at the same rope.'

Elizabeth: When the text was finalised, the graphic designer, Ruth Grüner, set to work. Ruth typeset the manuscript and then made all the 'documents' look as authentic as possible. Ruth's father came from Germany, so she asked him to do the German handwriting.

All this happened because Heike was game enough to come to Australia. She took a chance that it would work out, and it did.

Acknowledgements

This is a work of fiction but we adapted historical documents to create a feeling of authenticity.

The authors would like to thank Rosalind Price and Sue Flockhart at Allen & Unwin; Dame Nellie Melba Kindergarten Committee for providing the perfect place to work; designer Ruth Grüner for her skill and patient professionalism; those who contributed handwriting: Leo Pollmar (Leo), Karl Leister (Konrad), Jörn Grüner (Leopold), Sadie Richey (Gilly Kneebone); and Jens-Uwe Thomas of the Flüchtlingsrat Berlin for his information about refugees; Juliet O'Conor, Children's Literature Librarian, State Library of Victoria; and finally Dr Gisela Böhnhardt for help in a hundred ways: suggestions, meals, computer expertise and photography.

Thank you also to Dieter Kramer for use of the reproduction postcard from the period; and to Tom, for the cartoon *Touché*.

The Victorian Reading Book, Class II   Published by George Robertson & Co. 1907(?), Melbourne, Sydney, Adelaide and Brisbane, Adam and Charles Black, London, from the Children's Research Collection, State Library of Victoria

This reader is a precursor to the Victorian Readers later used in state schools, and gives a clear impression of the period, what children learned and how.

German book with photo of the *Zieten*   Arnold Kludas, *Die Seeschiffe des Norddeutschen Lloyd 1857–1919*, Koehlers Verlagsgesellschaft, Hamburg 1991

The story of the huge shipping line Norddeutscher Lloyd is extraordinary. Each world war they went broke. The *Zieten* is a story in itself.

***Zieten* Passengers' List**   Public Record Office Victoria, inward unassisted shipping – foreign ports. Fiche 454, 8 and 451, 4

It was a thrill to find the passengers lists of the *Zieten*, and a convenient Miss Schmidt we could cut and paste. Except for the addition of the Schmidt family and the deletion of blank space to make the document fit on the page, the list is as it was in the original.

FIRE CLAIMS FOUR LIVES newspaper report   Designer Ruth Grüner compiled a typical newspaper clipping from the time, using material from a copy of the *Age*, 1910. The report mirrors the language and issues of the time.